Leon Rooke

D1553211

LONG
TALKING
BAD CONDITIONS
BLUES

BOOKS BY RONALD SUKENICK

Long Talking Bad Conditions Blues
98.6
Out, a novel
The Death of the Novel and Other Stories
Up, a novel
Wallace Stevens: Musing the Obscure

LONG
TALKING
BAD CONDITIONS
BLUES

by
Ronald Sukenick

FICTION COLLECTIVE, INC. △ NEW YORK

Cover by Bobi Haldeman and Ed Huston.

Grateful acknowledgement is made to the magazines *Granta,
Luna Park,* and *Ploughshares,* in which portions of this novel first
appeared.

The publication of this book is in part made possible with
support from the National Endowment for the Arts, the Commit-
tee on University Scholarly Publications of the University of
Colorado at Boulder, and the New York State Council on the
Arts; and with the cooperation of the Teachers and Writers
Collaborative (New York) and the Department of English of the
University of Washington at Seattle.

First Edition

Copyright © 1979 by Ronald Sukenick
All rights reserved
Library of Congress Catalog No. 79-52030
ISBN: 0-914590-60-X (hardcover)
ISBN: 0-914590-61-8 (paperback)

Published by FICTION COLLECTIVE, INC.
Production by Coda Press, Inc.
Distributed by: George Braziller, Inc.
                One Park Avenue
                New York, N.Y. 10016

for Adek

from his apartment on Ferrell Anderson Place he liked to walk down to the quai which the local inhabitants referred to as The Reiser for reasons Carl was not able to determine but he somehow always lost his way on the way and found himself in a puzzle of winding and oblique streets complicated intersections which were not in themselves unpleasant in fact he would invariably find a series of book stalls an area of shops a neighborhood of fascinating if unpretentious architecture so that he would soon forget his original destination while absorbed in browsing through a collection of early Rhodesian medical texts or a group of mementos from the 1923 World Cup or speculating on the origins of a variation in the style of dormer windows in regional balloon frame houses at first he would often ask directions from policemen or at news stands but he understood the local turn of speech badly and spoke it even less well since he was never able to master the accent and rhythm finally it occurred to him that the crucial thing was detail and that the kind of detail did not much matter so he concentrated on that as he wandered through the streets addressing his fumbling questions to the natives famous for their impatience with strangers usually getting nowhere if not happily at least quite absorbed and he found if he paid attention sometimes he would stumble on a real find like the time he wandered into a club in Newcomb Alley to discover that Kenny Clarke was the featured artist though unfortunately it was Monday the day they always interrupted the regular schedule to host a miscellaneous collection of third rate locals and he was never able to find his way back to the place again even with the help of a city map he gave in and bought for the absurd price of five balls which he found useless due to its inaccuracy capricious scale and tiny print he eventually gave it to his girlfriend in the hope she would get lost the problem with Charleen and first of all he could never tolerate her name even in the early days when they were very much in love was not so much that she was unfaithful though that in fact was not something that bothered him in fact he fundamentally approved since it coincided with his ideas such as they were maybe it would be better to call them attitudes since they weren't very well thought out on a theoretical basis but this was no accident either since one of his ideas or attitudes was that he didn't believe in ideas abstraction went against his nature he would leave out his yet people change do they not but unfortunately Charleen was one of those who did not however much he reasoned and pleaded or crapped away the night in vicious arguments at the end of which the birds chirping and nothing settled he would swear he was leaving her for good but never got around to it maddened exhausted and hungry they would eat some kippers and bread drink a little schnapps and coca cola a drink they hade invented in The Smiling Lemming on Ferrell Anderson Place go to bed make love and start all over again the next day getting up usually around one or two in the afternoon disgusted with themselves and with each other and with the room which was strewn with dirty clothing bread crumbs cigarette butts and bits of kipper and at such moments he wished most of all he had a cat and over coffee he would once more try to explain to her very patiently that unfaithfulness he could accept it was fine it was possibly even desirable but that unfaithfulness combined with crazed and vicious jealousy was hard to take and that her obstinate refusal to admit its existence did not advance the discussion and then he would try to find his way usually unsuccessfully to Veronica's place whose name he at least liked and with whom he could at least talk if only at the level of harmless drivel but would often digress into a gallery or perhaps dreamily get involved in watching a good pick-up basketball game in Robinson Square Park but he never worried because he knew he was always bound to meet either Charleen or Veronica or one of his three friends in some

coffee place or bar or at one of the galleries or in a
bookstore or at The Reiser watching the ships come and go
or on a bench feeding the squirrels and at those moments
it was not a bad life he would think though at others he was
completely dissatisfied and restless lamenting the destruction of the public toilets which in his previous visits to the
city had been landmarks as well as conveniences which
was so far the only step taken in a planned campaign of
urban renewal whose main result was citizens pissing in
the streets in corners against lamp posts like dogs while
the dogs disoriented by this sudden materialization of
strange scents looked disgruntled and confused and
caused him personally occasional slight discomfort which
though slight served as an unpleasant reminder of the
panic under the surface to which he pretended to be so
indifferent at such times he would head immediately for
the Boulevard Lavaggetto and lose himself in the nifty
shops where you could buy a silk tie for example for twenty-
five balls and that looked so much like such places
everywhere with attractive well dressed women on their
way to and from lunch with the lady friend the quick
noonie with the virile floor walker and back to the
executive office in the ad agency or with the muscular
international shipping magnate who belongs to the same
country club as the husband she will now telephone to say
she will be late or the hairdresser or the mildly pleasant
errand such as a wedding gift for a distant cousin or finding
out about a private school for the ten year old son or the
yearly checkup or the office high up above the street to
sign the contract while stock boys lounge against the walls
enjoying post-hamburger cigarettes as they pass and
looking at their legs not to mention the men in English cut
suits with greying sideburns smoking pipes and here he
would often turn at the only right angled intersection in
the center of the city onto a wooded avenue with gravelled
pedestrian paths called The Walker where he would often

find Victor on a bench feeding the squirrels or pigeons and culling inflictions sometimes from the passersby sometimes from himself for example he might wear some outlandish article of clothing that would draw hoots and whistles from the pedestrians a boot on his arm say or a glove on his foot or feathers in elaborate and spectacular compositions on his head or hanging around his neck and would then attempt to engage his hecklers in reasoned discourse on the subject usually beginning with I'm from California the promised land and quickly launching from there into abstractions well beyond the ken of the man in the street with whom in fact he happened of necessity to be talking who not only misunderstood but was genuinely confused and embarrassed and tried his best to be polite though with little success but this was Victor's acid way of being serious filling what he called the verbal hole with airy provocations which his friend now strolling toward him on the gravelled path considered a hole which could not be filled because it did not exist except through a quirk of language he himself having long since given up on explanations and contenting himself with predictions which were no less valid for him simply because they always turned out to be incorrect in fact if they turned out to be correct so what in the long run it was predicton as a mode that absorbed him like that squirrel on the ground would jump up on the bench next to Victor and present him with a petition in the name of all the squirrels in The Walker it didn't or Charleen would suddenly appear in a mood of contrition and admit her errors she didn't still these possibilities were inherent in the flow of language into the verbal hole and just as quickly out of it and someone had to take them into account trees grass benches an adolescent girl on horseback and the multiple velocities of phenomena circulating through the city otherwise going unattended in all their possibility and so lonely so isolated that was how he thought about his function in this place that of keeping everything company and in so doing felt himself assuaged yet it was all so unsatisfactory and he would often find himself on the quai at The Reiser contemplating seaweed its massy flux wishing for razor blades or a haircut thinking his friend Tony was right he should shave his beard and initiate a five year plan but sometimes of course he would get into bright colors plastic reds and acid greens and neon pinks and the cows would start mooing in his head satisfying long drawn deep belly moos just this side of desperation where basso breaks to soprano like an adolescent boy who gets too excited perhaps on the way to the slaughterhouse and he would know it was time to get away from seaweed however attractive and lose himself in one of the streets winding off Kirby Higbe Place maybe following one of the skinny cats curving down Casey Street until he was overcome with the decadence of this kind of operation thinking the imposition of logic on seaweed thinking winding and oblique streets thinking his footsteps on the pavement disappearing behind him like progressive deletion as it began to rain or more like a heavy drizzle and the pedestrians on narrow Casey Street bumping one another with their black umbrellas and droplets on the skins of the autos like perspiration and the brows of the autos mopped by windshield wipers thinking who if not he would attend the petty iconography of the quotidian the texture of our days which is their meaning if any which unattended grows so lonely so forlorn and then turns back on us the portion we allot to it in a kind of sad appeal for help like the silent stubbornness of a discontented child or a dog shitting on the floor meaning by its disobedience the concept alienation that is starting with us and bouncing back from it skirting for example an industrial suburb early in the morning as the garbage truck works its way down the street just after the workers have left for the factory and the local dentist prepares his instruments for the first swollen face of the day perhaps a housewife up all night with the pain who after filling her man's lunch box comes to the office with her two brats aged three and five the latter a boy because she has no place to leave them her lids red and heavy and rings around her eyes in the shapeless house dress she carelessly wrapped around herself after drying her hands on the dish towel but still kind of sexy and the dentist thinks young wife telling her to relax as he injects the novocaine oh horny bachelor of wooden fences and neighborhood back yards with an occasional rabbit hutch whose practice includes certain industrial contracts or otherwise he would certainly be downtown where you can bet he lives or maybe it's just a routine cleaning and check up say the Swedish janitor from the next building always stinking of booze all this would come to mind walking through the drizzle of the outskirts back from the harbor thinking of the obligations of observation though and now he contradicts himself but gently since both things are true in a way it was never observation but always invention and even prophecy as in the two senses of the word witness and for that matter of the word prophecy language you might say is god's witness of the witless if you subtract the word god and take witless in the root sense but enough said he had no taste for prophecy and was content to be a camera without film the very presence of the camera being in his mind monitor enough to establish the integrity of certain blocks of data and if somebody wanted to go and climb the mountain okay his obligation ended with its notation which seemed to him at least as important since you can't climb a mountain before it is there and it was always always the simple thereness that was being slighted that was so hard to come at and yet so basic that he was sometimes inclined to think in moments of cheesy bravado that the documentation of this very thereness was itself the prophetic act taking the word documentation as more than half mentation and this was true he held not only for things in space but of curves of things through time that is to say all our little stories the ones that sometimes very occasionally reach the status of articulation of filler in the newspaper or at best human interest while City Hall's official version of life compiled by some bored clerk or statistician roughly on the basis of crude figures highly modified by political necessity and mostly conditioned by the remnants of Victorian novels floating through his underdeveloped imagination like surprising things at the bottom of yesterday's chicken soup steals the headlines which say nothing of the actual smoke of the actual stacks of the factory where his friend Tony works as a supervisor on an assembly line producing thermal units for electric ovens or of the subtleties of lunch hour in the canteen the ennuis of coke machines and powdered coffee the joys of the first hungry bites of salami sandwich the taste of bland mustard or the sour belches of afternoon coffee breaks or the exhilarations of four oclock racing to the bus stop or the parking lot into the absolute freedom of traffic jams the radio pounding heavy rock three fast beers and the box of drumsticks from Uncle Chicken the news on TV and then maybe a flick a bar maybe Veronica who was not after all going steady but screwing around in a mild way who knows what might happen till it was time for a few shots of Early Times before setting the fucking alarm clock and hitting the fucking sack oh lord but Tony could take care of himself it was Victor he would worry about and sometimes Victor's mother would call him in tears about her son's strange letters since he split with Charleen and he would feel a certain responsibility not only because Victor was his friend but especially because he was now living with Charleen and he would try to talk to Charleen about it but she didn't want to think about the bastard that's why she kicked him out so she wouldn't have to think about him anymore so then he would meet Victor in the bar in Camilli Lane called The Tartine and they would have a few and Victor would start talking about verbal holes and after a while he would start talking about carnal wholes and occasionally he would get into arguments with the customers about old baseball players but when he started bugging the bartender to shut the asshole TV off because he wanted to have a serious discussion about California where everything was different and why not why shouldn't it be he knew it was time to get him out of the bar fast because first of all he knew that Victor had never been to California and also that when he started talking about it he could get very hostile though otherwise Victor's growing eccentricity was in the direction of excessive sweetness an almost unearthly generosity of spirit something quite angelic really to the point where he would neglect his own welfare to accommodate any stranger's slightest whim just keep him away from California and verbal holes and also what he called the sexual impasse which would always drive him into an incoherent frenzy of pugnacious invective directed at whoever happened to be around get it back to the 1939 Detroit Tigers as quickly as possible the trouble was that this evening the fellow at the bar next to them went into a pugnacious frenzy about the 1939 Detroit Tigers and a bad fight was barely avoided mostly by the bartender an ex cop kicked off the force for brutality which in this town must really have been brutal who suddenly got red in the face and told them look you guys quiet down or I'll bust both your fuckin heads but these angelic eccentricities of the soul were insufficient and certainly not decisive in the struggle for more lucid days or reluctant acquiescence in the fine cold mist that settled on the city these winter months since if lucidity were desirable which was itself a question it seemed doubtful it would be so all the time and so there was a kind of dialogue here between mist and sun that was at the heart of the season with the grey buildings either smudged in with charcoal the outlines always slightly blurred and everything a little out of focus a little vague in general aspect though clear enough in detail unless one made a concentrated effort which he consciously declined to make in hope of finding satisfaction with things as they were if that was the way they were but that was a decision he had made and was inclined to see it through otherwise how would he know if it was correct or too sharp and cold too piercing as he put it and he stayed in the house and so we find him taking notes on dog shit in Owen Road and garbage cans in Preacher Row yeck you well might say but there was logic to this Bensonhurst of apprehension fabricated with each step with no regrets and occasional deep satisfaction despite his growing conviction that Charleen was not merely different but possibly a demented lunatic whatever he might want to say in favor of the fecundity of chronic distraction rendering observation of the ragged peripheries so acute it amounted to a new definition of the center and why not accept these limits he would think the limitations of glinting facets of happy ambiguities of fascinating door knobs the texture of pizzas the feathering of ear lobes the lesser gestures of sea anemones complaints of clams gesticulation of sea weed torpor of sidewalks hullaballoo of slugs gleam of jet planes smudge of stacks rain drops bridge work tin cans knees streets sighs curves sheets the clarity of persistent ellipsis the logic of lacunae the facile discords of discontinuity thinking at the same time the phrase maddeningly local and at such times the whole city would present itself in terms of dotted lines implying a possible city behind the city that possibly wasn't there a code concocted by an idiot suffering from progressive aphasia but not after all so different from J. Robert Oppenheimer her idea being the incorporation of vague peripheries in fructive systems but if the systems themselves were merely one shot intersections what then their domestic harangues would often turn on this but what was the point of life he would often ask himself in the icy silence that followed one of these jagged debates it was the creation of social textures by discrete groups in which the individual could satisfy his physical needs and his desires varying grossly from person to person for ego gratification without excessive frustration but with enough to allow for the fullest exercise of his capacities and in fact to encourage it in ratio to the group's need for productivity or so he would frequently speculate then what was all the fuss about it was about contradictions among these various specifications among individuals among different groups between groups and individuals such as would arise according to circumstance it was about changes in circumstance that shattered patterns it depended on the rate of shatter and the kind of shatter for example there might well be some kinds of shatter that various individuals might feel it was not worth adapting to no matter what their rates of adaptation and there was another problem too and that was adaptation to what circumstance since circumstance is often difficult to apprehend or worse there might be several circumstances adaptation to which might not be completely compatible and then it was not only a question of adaptation but of what adaptation since appropriate adaptations are not all that easy to come by and that immediately brings up the question of where adaptations come from luck careful analysis delirious invention all of these and more and if so in what medium and that brings up the question of medium and whether there is a basic medium and whether it can be said that medium implies articulation and whether the basis of articulation does not no matter how you want to labor it come back to language as terminal in both senses of the word of all the sense and senses intersection of necessity and invention then the thing would be to be most in touch with these from the point of view of change which probably however puts you out of touch with what you're changing from so that you find yourself saying hello before you have a chance to wave goodbye that was the kind of problem Carl had with Charleen who had an extremely accelerated rate of change though in this she was merely exemplary of individuals in a period of accelerated shatter and it was also the kind of problem Victor had with Charleen since from Victor's point of view it was he who had walked out on Charleen saying hello to new circumstance before he was able to say goodbye to the old and the consequent guilt went a long way toward explaining why Victor was so intent on culling infliction and furthermore Victor had the impression that his body was broken up in parts and that was the reason that he had left Charleen in the first place because he had become incapable of flow due to multiple blockage which he blamed on Charleen but can one ever blame this sort of thing on another Victor was aware of the question and his answer was a tentative yes and it was true that Charleen had also stopped flowing but she blamed this on Victor but it was also true that Charleen had a tendency to what Carl called spasmic flow meaning either total blockage or flow to overflow the overflow sooner or later leading to total blockage and that Victor had a tendency to break down into constituent parts or what Carl called sector flow because one sector could flow independently of another sector for example visual flow apart from mental flow or emotional flow apart from sexual flow and how would he characterize his own kind of flow Carl would often wonder idly watching the pedestrians in Ferrell Anderson Place from his window or pacing along The Reiser and he was never able to decide beyond arriving at some general conclusions such as that for example it was almost impossible to come to a conclusion about one's own flow and that in fact this was a contradiction in terms since one was precisely one's own flow so that conclusion was impossible and even undesirable whatever the culture might recommend about being objective having perspective and that however flow was not entirely personal but also between persons and had to do with synchronic rhythms and that lack of synchronic rhythms had a lot to do with the so-called sexual impasse which had a lot to do with carnal wholes and that carnal wholes when interrupted by blockage had a lot to do with verbal holes which implied a blockage of articulation due to accelerated shatter so that one thing was no longer connected with another but when he would try to explain this to Tony over a beer Tony would say something like if it's all so simple then how come you aren't rich which was to the point in a way but then he would immediately turn this around for the benefit of Charleen if she happened to be there and who was in fact rich and would ask her in that case if you're so rich how come you aren't simple since the opportunities the word rich implied certainly included that of attaining his favorite virtue but Charleen would characteristically respond that is to say whether she were there or weren't it didn't matter fuck off you don't understand anything which was probably true though if he understood anything at all he thought he understood a few things about flow and the rhythm of flow which was always changing and always had to change come what may via new departures from the terminal of language and about the direction of flow which was into itself like a sea although he would reflect staring at the sea weed from the dock on The Reiser who was he to make comments about the sea and the hazy sea which resembled a thin opaque soup as it rose to slosh against the ambiguous grey rim of the horizon would not give away any secrets

then one day it was spring and everything seemed to resolve into emerging units   one emerging unit was Veronica and Drecker the dentist who started appearing very frequently   he started appearing very frequently at The Same Thing their new hangout but why   why became clear when they noticed he would show each time Veronica would no others   the others were amazed because Drecker was the only one there not a confirmed goofoff   Drecker was a goofoff but not a confirmed goofoff like Victor and Tony say   confirmed goofoffs had no aims no expectations no hopes and liked it that way   Carl's own vague wanderings and meditations aimless as they were fit into the category   no one else had anything resembling an excuse for being alive except Drecker   Drecker's excuse that is pulling teeth though admittedly flimsy qualified him as a separate unit   now with spring Drecker felt an organic need to synchronize himself with creation   the nearest handy part of it was Veronica and her friends and their unit   Drecker envisaged himself and Veronica as a subunit in fact they were one already   before Veronica had joined the unit she had gone to see Drecker with a toothache   Drecker pulled the tooth and they immediately became lovers but it was a bad start   Veronica wasn't sure whether the relationship was based on pleasure or relief of pain   there were other difficulties Drecker lived on Casey Street famous for its carefree bums   these bums were a source of annoyance to Drecker he never gave them any money   perhaps because of this they always heckled him on his way to his door   also they liked to gather under his window for impromptu drunken serenades of unprecedented cacaphony   Veronica on the other hand was always throwing them coins or urging Drecker to   while Drecker made love to her she would lose herself in digging their boozy chorales   Veronica claimed their singing was surprisingly atonal a remark she often repeated always irritating Drecker   when Drecker expressed his irritation she would sulk or say something imperious and final   sometimes she would stop in the middle of lovemaking with remarks that drove Drecker nuts   the worst of these was I want you to make me a cup of tea   when she said that their subunit was dissolved for the rest of the day   it was predictable that their subunit would terminate quickly and in fact it did   but evidently the attraction re-emerged among the unifications of spring when emerging units merge   did spring make Drecker recognize the isolation of his life among the professional cadres   maybe the warm wind recalled to him from childhood how sweet it was to do nothing   maybe it was the subtle influence of the bums under his window on Casey Street   in any case he gave up tennis and started goofing off with Veronica's goofoff friends   in March the wind came off the sea bringing gusts of warm rain   the clouds went wild in front of a full moon over Ferrell Anderson Place   in The Same Thing Drecker was telling Veronica nice guys don't win pennants   Carl came in as Veronica was arguing with Drecker that she wasn't a pennant   he told Drecker that was undoubtedly true but maybe Charleen was a pennant   Veronica said yes because he wasn't a nice guy she felt sorry for Charleen   Carl said he felt sorry for himself because Charleen was being strange again   you see Veronica said he should feel sorry for Charleen maybe so he said   Carl meant being nice was no good either with Charleen total lack of affect continued   Drecker who liked talking about units said maybe she was a self contained unit   Victor came in and said he definitely agreed we are all units what kind   we are all units of production and consumption in the technology of postindustrial culture   we are all bits of information in bytes of data mutually incommunicado collectively excommunicated   thus verbal holes he said returning to his obsession gulfs within and gulfs without   the sophistications of technology are no improvement on the mystifications of personality said Charleen   she whipped through the door like someone with something mean on her mind

like a beer Carl asked my my aren't you the gentle-
man tonight Charleen answered   what's eating you
I'm tired of living on an island she snapped that's all
      you have cabin fever you don't need to live in a cabin
said Victor   really she said who asked you I want a beer
I want to leave   Tony appeared and played Hotel
California on the jukebox the others tapped in rhythm
      Charleen twitched her ass like a rattlesnake in heat
she got a lethal bored expression   she had the look of
somebody about to kill somebody for the fun of it   can
I join you asked Tony I'm just about to leave she said
      she didn't move you're a down hill trip all the
way said Tony   every time I look at you I get a
bellyache he added   if you have problems said Charleen take them elsewhere she never liked Tony   she
would tell Carl Tony was garbage playing on his last name
which was Garbaggio   Charleen made such a point of
disliking Tony he assumed she really like Tony   Tony
fed the pinball machine a couple of coins jerking violently
at the levers   you could be politer Carl said what do I
care what you think said Charleen   he could hear the
mooing in his head again the scene shimmered in a
mirror   we could go out in my boat Drecker told
Charleen Veronica looked peeved   oh said Charleen
right now not at night said Drecker tomorrow with the
tide   look out Veronica said Victor am I doing something wrong asked Charleen let's go now   you know I
get seasick Carl said yes I know she said stay home   if
Carl's not going I'm not going said Veronica who invited
you asked Victor   let's go now said Charleen why not I
don't know said Drecker at night   Charleen doesn't
understand why not said Victor weird gaps in consciousness perforated with verbal holes   I'm none of your
business anymore said Charleen who managed Detroit in
1947 asked Victor   maybe tomorrow with the tide said
Drecker I'm not going said Veronica are you   we'll see

Carl said that night he and Charleen fought over the boat   making love was like a continuation of the struggle by other means hard nasty   Charleen didn't come and they had another fight over that neither of them slept   Carl got up in the morning in a state of intense depression she of anger   she told him he was the worst lover she ever had cold mechanical unimaginative   she said he was a lousy conversationalist incredibly boring cold fish moved like a robot   she said she was making coffee and eggs for herself he could make his own   he said she was incredibly petty uptight middle class trying to be bohemian   he said if she couldn't get her head together don't blame it on others   he said she was whacked out on too much acid basically a mean bitch   she said she didn't care what he thought she lacked respect for him   she said she didn't love him there was no longer any question about that   she said she didn't know how she could have made such a big mistake   he said she made a lot of mistakes because she wasn't too bright   she only looked intelligent and on top of that she was crazy and cheap   and if she didn't like him she should send for money and get out   because he'd had it up to here she said she was through she was leaving   as soon as she got some money he said he couldn't wait nor I   she added immediately he said good I'm going out for breakfast good she said   he went out for coffee smoked five cigarettes was furious wished he had a cat   but he told himself at least he knew he was at ground zero   where everyone else seemed to be he was in The Smiling Lemming at the counter   Victor came in Victor started talking about the sexual impasse shut up Carl said   he told Victor a change was coming he didn't know what but it was coming   when you're at ground zero it has to come who knows maybe for the worse   the mooing in his head confirmed all suspicions including disintegration of

phenomena including verbal holes   when he went
back upstairs Charleen said she had been dreaming of
rats   and other horrible animals on the floor does that
tell you anything he asked   it tells me I'm worried she
said what about my lovers are coming she said   here to
the island he asked how many of them are there seven or
eight   seven or eight you've got to be kidding you
mean just during Christmas vacation   well it was a long
vacation besides I'm not sure one was a woman   does
that count she asked maybe seven just counting the men
more or less   it's odd once you open a little bit they all
come jamming in   and they were all so beautiful she
said with a dreamy high school look   wasn't there a
traffic control problem I never slept with more than two a
day   maybe three sometimes depending who I spent
the night with it was a cataclysm   again the swoony
look of a teenager getting off on a rock star   so you
finally made it he said most popular cunt in town good
work   none of those relations were cheap or promis-
cuous she snapped you can cheapen anything   there
was a long period of silence they didn't talk for about an
hour   it had a quality of mutual stasis imposed by each
on the other   the brutal sound of a pneumatic drill her
hands in her lap childish hopeless   there are only two
kinds of power he said love and money I have neither
       Carl predicted that the left would take over in the
next election and that this would do nothing to resolve the
island's current political impasse incoherence and lack of
direction   on the contrary it would only deepen the
confusion and it would be clear to all that this only
represented a transition phase but transition to what
       the new situation would be nothing more than a
crystallization of the agitated stasis of the old situation that
is politics degree zero weird lapse of civic consciousness   meanwhile out in the countryside the cows

would still come home the tractors would still send long trails of dust drifting behind them mechanization increasingly depopulating the farms   the cities would continue to fill with surplus labor and would continue to go broke the middle classes would continue their movement to the peripheries nothing would change   according to Victor the proposed leftist coalition between the PPS and the PTE was only a repetition of the politics of the popular front and was by its very nature ineffectual   in fact there was also a proposed coalition between the PPS and the CRU on the right which would be just as plausible according to Victor's ongoing analysis   Victor was of the opinion that only the hopelessly naive considered the current maneuvering anything more than a tactic to disguise the manipulations of international super financial intelligence powers   Carl told Victor it would be a comfort to believe that there was someone in charge who knew what they were doing at least Victor said hopelessly naive   Victor said the international super financial intelligence powers controlled one's life down to the most intimate details he said that verbal holes were no accident just for example   Victor said verbal holes were the consequence of intelligence withheld by super financial powers power being really a question of information and without information one could simply not think   this fait accompli was then incorporated into the current ideology people were encouraged instead to feel and in fact they could not do otherwise and made a virtue of necessity   mumbling became the style intentional incoherence discontinuity ending in a virtual celebration of autism whole populations were held incommunicado agents planted in the media discouraged reading encouraged self expression   the revolution of rising expectations had to be stopped production slows consumption is diminished growth cut back population control encouraged ecology popularized small becomes

beautiful do it yourself   goal orientation is minimized
dropping out is maximized hedonism is sanctioned sex is
liberated abortion is legalized zero population growth is
advanced family is discouraged mating is for fun   pro-
miscuity becomes stylish is pushed in the media women
are liberated especially from childbirth bisexuality is chic
Charleen gets strung out on her lovers to help reduce the
surplus labor force   the sexual impasse is upon us
marriage doesn't work liberation doesn't work heterosex-
uality doesn't work homosexuality doesn't work promis-
cuity doesn't work chastity doesn't work love is old
fashioned   a cold narcissism prevails all that remains is
improving oneself but nobody knows for what self realization getting your head together getting clear getting off on
yourself   Carl and Victor were in The Smiling Lemming
on Ferrell Anderson Place they decided to see what was
happening at The Same Thing strolling down Lavaggetto to
Wyatt   it was lunch time Wyatt was quiet shops closed
citizens home or in small hotels with their lovers the
restaurants were crowded he felt adrift he thought of
Drecker's boat   he thought if you're going to live on
an island it's a good idea to have a boat so you don't get to
feeling isolated avoid cabin fever   though living on
the island was itself like being on a boat he often felt afloat
here detached adrift it was not totally unpleasant nor
totally pleasant either   he always felt a little seasick
that is a little disoriented but in fact it was no different from
the way he felt when he was on the mainland   it was
the condition of things the general disorientation and
underlying disquiet you might even say panic the uncer-
tainty about the future and maybe worse about the
past   the assassinations and the rigged elections and
the phony wars or the wars that were real but for phony
reasons the fluctuations in the currency the sudden short-
ages   the disastrous surpluses while nobody had
enough these things were the same on the island or off

the constant unemployment at a time when nobody could find enough workers   which reminded him that he needed a job he was running out of money out of money Charleen was going to pieces his life was disintegrating how unpleasant   and yet the life on the island was not unpleasant courage is panic on deposit he told Victor accumulating interest in The Same Thing Veronica was eating lunch   she was alone she just had a fight with Drecker who wanted to pull some of her teeth and give her braces why can't we leave well enough alone she asked

we're all spoiled and have to make life interesting for ourselves said Victor it's the price of narcissism lack of commitment fragmented community torpid intellect funny attitudes soggy language   ah can you loan me a little **money till my next check comes asked Victor as they were** about to order why don't you get a job Carl answered

what said Victor I don't fit in anywhere said Victor **nobody fits in anywhere Carl said anymore not even people who have jobs he said**   right on said Veronica who worked as a waitress in The Tartine I once had plenty of money said Victor more money than I knew what to do with   I was trading in futures I couldn't do anything wrong the money kept coming in I just happened to be in the right place at the right time   I knew what it was all about I pronounced on things with all the moral authority of someone who's happened to discover an oil well in his back yard   at the same time I'd do things like a girlfriend demanded a present she gave me a choice so I bought a stuffed goat and had it reupholstered with fur   when I gave it to her she said what's that I said you asked for a mink goat no coat she screamed that little joke cost five thousand   it was Charleen who talked me out of futures she said there was no future in them she said the **whole idea of the future was completely passé   def-initely unhip you had to** live in the moment and the best place to live in the moment was on an island because space equals time you see   no said Veronica well if space equals time then living in a finite here equals living in a finite now anyway civilization is going nowhere from here right   at best Carl said so let's live a little said Veronica you goofoffs said Drecker who just came in it's a transition phase whole new units are emerging   stop with the units already said Veronica what's the matter with you he's not himself said Victor and he never was I just heard the boat I came on sank   and the boat I came on last time sank eerie said Veronica it's as if something's after you I think there's something after all of us said Victor   maybe it was to get away from it they had each come to the island Carl thought the island with its trees so much like the trees at home   the old city with its complicated network of streets at the bottom then above that the skyscrapers the office buidlings then the slums to the west the fields the farms   the man in the next apartment continued to beat his dog which continued to piss in the hall the currency continued to fluctuate and his research went nowhere   Carl had gotten a grant for coming to the island to study a kind of personality able to cope with the vicissitudes and complications of the new conditions   the island was thought to be the best area for such field work because it manifested the whole complex of circumstances generally referred to as the new conditions   the most salient feature of the new conditions was that they were extremely hard to grasp thus he made the case in his grant application for the island   the case consisted of the argument that the new conditions would be easier to grasp in a limited space but this did not prove to be the case   because the problem was not bringing into consciousness things that already existed in some other realm like Freud but things that wouldn't exist until they were brought into it   and so where was one to begin his only model was clouds their resolution in the sky their subtle transitions from nothing to something in the empty air   the way they massed over the mountains at noon blackened the city sky orchestrating the lives of the citizens with passing but awesome force leaving its indelible effect then   then over the ocean at sunset pink and spent assuming shapes that redefine the beautiful but only after the fact arguing that beauty is power in retrospect   though there was something to his project after all in that there were certain clear physical correspondences here to the new conditions for example the frequent gaping holes   these were areas that had been razed some years ago in strategic parts of the city at a time when ambitious civic projects had been planned and commissioned   whole blocks had been demolished populations relocated then between demolition and construction the original plans had been found inadequate or wrongheaded or too expensive or unpropitious for the times   these gaping holes as they were generically called had gradually become part of the normal landscape the politicians were constantly proposing new schemes for them which were clearly unworkable   the citizens referred to them with affectionate irony and they had even become proverbial as in the saying necessary as a gaping hole or fraught with gaping holes   thus the odd gaps in consciousness concerning the new conditions and the curious lacunae in the conditions themselves were visibly manifest in these civic ellipses and confused stalemates

the vague irony about the holes was itself symptomatic of the citizens' dissatisfaction with the government and its policies and with politics in general which had no outlet   occasionally there would be a spasm of public outrage when for example a small child would fall into a hole and disappear and there would be a recall election

or when a politician would advance a particularly absurd or self serving hole proposal parking garages made of transparent cement monumental pyramids constructed by a brother-in-law's monumental pyramid company

actually he found the gaping hole in his neighborhood fascinating though he would get annoyed when Charleen referred to it as a found earthwork masterpiece

of the minimalist school   he would stare into the hole
for hours pondering its double nature it was there and not
there its absence an apparition called forth only by
surrounding presence   it seemed a mirror image of
the phenomena of the quotidian whose presence after
contemplating the hole struck him as an apparition called
forth only by surrounding absence   if so his intuition
of the city as a complex of dotted lines traced in by tacit
though unrealized agreement of the citizens might be a
legitimate hypothesis   further research might indicate
that realization of the unrealized agreement might lead to
conscious choice in the way the dotted lines were traced
altering the outlines of the city   thus realization of the
unrealized by surrounding its presence with revealing
absence might lead to a better adaptation to the new
conditions through altering the new conditions themselves   or it might lead to eruption of the fear underlying the nostalgic ennui of coffee houses of small hotels
with their mediocre love affairs and panic in the
streets
                        acid green plastics red blobs stain vision
        sliding planes of grainy video fuschia mauve   phe-
nomena liquify and shimmer light fluctuates fades   sidewalks undulate beneath wavering shadows hydrants dis-
solve   Charleen continues sleeping sixteen hours a
day   wakes up nasty eats reads the dictionary   takes
mysterious notes crazy about the g's   what's with you
and Charleen asks Veronica   she's so terrific you're
such a pig   can you stand that bitch says Tony   to
love her is to know her   the mooing rises to a piercing
screech   police patrol streets in threes and fours
        ask for papers make citizens remove shoes   ru-
mors about obscene brutalities at police headquarters
        special torture rooms supervised by government
doctors   electric shock fingernails hot wax in their
        beating rape forced to drink their own   hung
upside down women bottles shattered in   genitals

teeth crushed families obliged to watch   no way to
prove to talk about   essential to new conditions or sick
aberration   as long as nobody's hungry said Charleen
       people furrowing through garbage in the slums
       possible sickness at center of new conditions   ex-
plaining lapse and stasis of civic energy   or was it
maybe transition evolution mutation   and if so was it
for the worse   impasse dark erotic forces attack generation itself   or panicked species seeking regenera-
tion through degeneration   pornographic frenzy of
thwarted libido corroding relations   on the other hand
islands get crazy   this is the well known island variable   isolation solipsism a factor researchers always
discount   though the island variable can be general
       a space time factor with broad social implica-
tions   isolation solipsism operating in a given epoch
       such periods are known as time islands   they
have the characteristics of geographical islands   alienation of a period from its past   insecurity about its
future separation from both   we live perhaps on such
an island   the condition repeated in each individual
separately   interiorization of external factors in help-
less repetition   citizens trapped in egos out of contact   no apprehension of causes or of consequences   unable to realize that life is real   unrealized
lives stunted in a perpetual adolescence   disillusion
with everything leads to vicious nihilism   everything is
tried and nothing gives satisfaction   the island variable
leads to dangerous despair   no psychosocial restraints
on an obscene barbarism   meanwhile the gay music
continues to play   street musicians out in the spring
weather   radios and stereos from doors and windows   the lottery the horses grow in popularity   all
games of chance enjoy a boom   citizens more fanatic
about sports if possible   sports heros have the status of
saints   streets are named after them cults started
       sports are assigned an almost religious purity

meanwhile religion is giving way to astrology   the
status of the occult rises constantly   what you can't
understand won't hurt you   and might help unlike
ordinary everyday ignorance   the incredible becomes
credible elsewhere cynicism prevails   public euphoria
grows despite kidnappings and terrorism   nostalgia
keeps the present out of focus
                                and yet the possibili-
ties   an island so rich   despite the starving slums
        Charleen their own fault   typical of her class
        yet the possibilities here   with planning with
technology   the mystifications of technology   the
island almost round   blue-green seen from above
        demographically perfect for investigations   a re-
searcher's dream it   tentative conclusions of previous   existence beyond his ego   proved by many
footnotes   collective solipsism impossible colleagues
        raw data from field   specialists confirm reliable
actualities   lucid verifications deny spontaneous
        speleologues of consciousness agree   determi-
nations consensus ineffable essentials   deliberations
on epistemological basis   inestimable calibrations insensible solutions
                        wrecked relations   bad dreams
        wasted semen   degenerated generation   sha-
ky nerves   phantasmal degradations   hollow voices   ephemeral phenomena   lost convictions
        abominable maledictions   terminal cruelties
        cheap tricks   quick lays   night sweats   time
drift   energy leak   emotional deprivation   insubstantial depravity   irretrievable loss   enervated
stasis

telling it like it is is the point of his research Carl says the reveries of the suburbs the actualities of the town included in the realities of the new conditions and their unrealities or as Charleen likes to say what is happening to us best then to admit the mysteries the blanks in consciousness on the principle that for every something there is an equivalent nothing that is at the same time part of the something that insensible x without which it could not exist let us then forget our fatuous infatuation with final fact and the continuities thereof since we are all figures on the ground of nothingness like the ghostly trees in Reese Park that grace the actual oaks with their swaying mass and relax with the pace of normal speech that depends on the normal silence of the listener

the listener in the small kiosk in the fine rain in the city's major park who answers that the submarine is getting too moist too claustrophobic and Carl realizes that Victor in fact has not been listening and has gone off the deep end again I was once with a man who was about to be hanged it was in a former British colony and he was being hanged with some others as an agent nothing could be done maybe he was an agent anyway he wanted to be with someone who spoke English and since I had a slight acquaintance with him they called me in I couldn't say no well he was remarkably cool while the others were praying he chatted away about everyday things in the last few minutes he got a little concerned and smoked a cigarette he told me he envisioned his death as a violently sexual dance only without a floor said Victor he was talking about his relation with Charleen

part of the new conditions was an uncontrollable multiplication of personal problems first of all relationships were breaking up on every side marriages families lovers friendships no one could seem to sustain a relationship for more than two days marriages of fifteen years dissolved overnight and everybody thought it was everybody else's fault for example in this very same kiosk in Reese Park where Carl so much liked to come when he felt a need for a calm and old fashioned relation to nature just a few days ago Charleen was telling him what was happening to her was his fault don't blame me for fucking you up he told Charleen you fucked up yourself because you're a fuckup that's why you fuck up part of Charleen's problem was that she was what she called schizzy that is a circle without a center that is the peripheries didn't relate to anything but other peripheries if at all

everybody's problems Victor's latest problem was he thought he might be gay Tony didn't know what to do with his life Drecker felt guilty about everything Veronica wasn't sure she was a woman one day sitting in the kiosk in Reese Park alone Carl realized that he didn't have any problems except other people's problems and maybe an attachment to liquor cigarettes and grass and women if that was a problem now he thought he'd try to get rid of those if he got rid of those maybe he'd become a saint not that he wanted to become a saint but maybe that was a viable hypothesis for his research project maybe if there were a few saints around it would establish criteria maybe that was what was needed for the new conditions new criteria maybe a few saints would establish new criteria that one could then move in and out of in and out of in and out of total detachment new criteria for new conditions

Carl was waiting for Veronica in The Same Thing she was bringing information about a possible job he wanted a job for two reasons the most important was that he was running out of money and the second was he no longer liked being at home very much because of Charleen in fact he was glad he was meeting Veronica it was a relief Veronica was interesting she complained a lot but she was good at getting along if only at a primitive level getting along was something he was not good at at any level and he tended to admire people who were good at getting along Charleen was not good at getting along was brought up wealthy and accustomed to an economy of excess in all things including people use it and throw it away Veronica was better fit for the new economy of limited resources thrifty collage and bricolage perhaps this explained her relation with Bennett

Carl had made love with Veronica a couple of times part of the new conditions was that everybody had made love with everybody a couple of times it had been a matter of circumstance of geometry you might even say he had happened to be in The Tartine late one night when Veronica got off of work as she put it and he offered to walk her home it was just after the first time Veronica had broken up with Drecker and she was lonely Veronica had broken up with Drecker about four times already but this was after the first time part of the new conditions was that everybody kept breaking up with everybody and kept getting together again they were walking down The Walker toward Lavaggetto when Veronica suddenly said let's go down to The Reiser so they took the short cut through Herman and sat down on a bench on The Reiser it was an unusually balmy night the moon was rising over the ocean huge and perfectly full

need we go further no in any case now he decided he had
better find a job and that he had better learn from Veronica
or from someone how to get along if he wanted to be a
saint of the new conditions a saint of the conditional a
conditional saint Bennett was Veronica's husband with
whom she no longer lived almost everybody had a
husband or wife with whom they no longer lived you could
almost take it for granted in the new conditions with
everybody breaking up and getting together all the time
why bother getting divorced or married either for that
matter Bennett wrote reports that's how he got along now
Veronica said Bennett knew of another job writing reports
the reports it seemed had to do with maternity Carl said he
didn't know anything about maternity Veronica told him
he didn't need to know about maternity it was just a matter
of handling information she said Bennett said

Bennett said you didn't have to know anything about the

information you were handling if you knew how to handle it and that furthermore one school of thought maintained that you could handle the information better if you didn't know anything about it because it left you less cluttered since it was all a matter of processing and you didn't want inert clots of knowledge impeding the information flow inert clots of knowledge furthermore could lead to the rigid form of humanistic intelligence known as wisdom which was nothing more than information frozen in traditional cliches which were completely inappropriate to the new conditions which were fluid atraditional and constantly changing and ossified the cybernetics of the mind which was a digital process dealing in a progressive minutia of yesno determinations

yesno determinations according to Bennett could only function in a value free mental ambiance and nothing could be more antithetical to the bright yesno clarities of the new thought than the vague and foggy meanderings of the humanistic perhaps she said Bennett said Carl turned this over in his mind he reminded himself that on the one hand Bennett was a confirmed exile who hadn't left the island for ten years and therefore might be out of touch but that on the other hand that Bennett knew how to write reports and that furthermore Bennett knew how to get along and that on the whole perhaps Bennett was correct but that then again perhaps he was not though he imagined and admired Bennett's clear silvery yesno mental atmosphere filled with flashing red and green lights he imagined a thought going through Bennett's head must be like a ball going through a pinball machine

Carl and Charleen were already doing the laundry in the bathtub and buying powdered milk he was down to one brick and four or five hundred balls which wasn't much because of the inflation he had obliquely suggested to Charleen that she take a part time job in the quote escort service he felt it was work she would be good at and that she would enjoy and he couldn't think of anything else she could do Veronica had done it from time to time and said it wasn't so bad depending it was mostly with tourists but what Charleen thought of this idea never emerged from the still black pool of her consciousness he thought of borrowing money from Drecker he went over to The Tartine where Drecker was hanging out because Veronica worked there The Tartine was pretty much a working

man's place and Drecker would hang out there with Tony
both of them wearing leather working man's caps

unlike The Smiling Lemming which was for tourists and
The Same Thing which was very local The Tartine was
patronized by a cross section of the ethnic population of
the island which was extremely various especially since the
current influx of immigrant labor encouraged by the
employment agencies which in fact could not find enough
jobs so that these workers then had to be supported by the
state surrogate system aggravating already severe eco-
nomic difficulties and increasing conditions of urban misery
but improving the representative quality of the island for
purposes of research so that one could go to the The Tartine
and hear many different languages and see a vast array of
ethnic types which were quickly altering the cultural
nature of the island once considered dominantly anglo
saxon but now after many such waves of immigration on
the point of a new cultural amalgam

personally he preferred the international ambiance of The Smiling Lemming The Smiling Lemming was a bar known all over the world rock stars lunched there when they came to the island to give a performance at night they had music and they say The Beatles played there before they were famous after the fight between the singer and the Canadian Prime Minister which received international coverage the prices which were escalating due to inflation had shot out of sight but you could still get a beer or a cup of coffee for less than a ball and sit around all afternoon though the place had its drawbacks the tourists the contempt of the citizens for the tourists was legendary especially among those in the service industries this of course is true in any region with a sizable tourist trade but was no doubt aggravated here by the nature of the tourist attraction the tourist attraction of the island was by and large the citizens themselves who were known for their energy their style their animation the rugged attractiveness of the men the willowy beauty of the women and above all their famous indifference which created an atmosphere to which foreigners felt they could come and do what they had wanted to do but had never dared as long as no laws were broken so that the island was like a playground where you could realize your fantasies and as often as not you realized that your fantasies were the last thing you wanted to realize and that in fact they were fantasies because they were not realized since if they were they wouldn't be fantasies the question then was what to do with your fantasies and the answer was to use them as a kind of thought a kind of meditation that in certain ways was superior to ordinary thought

the fact that the citizens themselves were the main tourist attraction of the island no doubt exacerbated the normal tensions between tourists and natives the citizens cherished their privacy they did not like being on stage as it were for the tourists they felt it as a form of condescension in the guise of admiration they did not like the ways the tourists irresistibly it seemed imitated their ways sometimes even becoming more islander than the islanders yet never with any authenticity but with the result that the ways of the islanders would often begin to seem inauthentic to the islanders themselves they would begin to feel themselves as mere phantasmal projections of the touristic imagination and begin to lose the sense of their own reality as a result of the touristic sensibility whose projections were themselves the consequence of the tourists' inadequate conviction of their own reality

the result of tourism on the island then besides helping to support its economy was to produce a progressive fantasia which gave the illusion of a liberation of desire while creating immense confusions as to what was desirable but it amused him in a way to sit there in The Smiling Lemming watching the tourists writing their optimistic postcards home postcards that would never be delivered due to the decline of the postal service as a result of the endless stream of postcards that overloaded facilities and exas-

38

perated overworked personnel combined with the general
bad temper that had taken hold since the last war leading
to a sort of demoralized negligence among the working
class population many of whom had been soldiers even
though the islanders had been on the winning side a kind
of grumbling dissatisfaction international in scope which
strangely enough was most pronounced in the winning
countries

domestic conditions were degenerating they were usually
too angry to make love and that made them even angrier
Carl said he was going to have to find someone to make
love to Charleen said good go ahead she couldn't care less
she was completely cool about that he could sleep with
anyone he wanted so he told her about making love with
Veronica and she got furious he said but but but she said
she didn't give a damn about his sleeping with Veronica it
was that he was trying to use it against her to make her
jealous an incredibly cheap trick she was angry at the
cheapness of it she told him she was sleeping with Drecker
she told him she was going out with him on his boat she
told him they would get it on at least three times each trip
she told him Drecker was a terrific lover he said he was no

longer interested in her seedy life but she had better stay
away from his friends or else or else what

he was about to go off his head when the agent called and
told him not to go off his head and could he speak to
Charleen please he told Charleen they had told her not to
do this in the first place not to come to the island not to
move in with this boy not to sleep with Drecker that it was
time to grow up and calm down that there was a ticket
home waiting for her permanently at American Express
and that all she had to do was go and pick it up any time she
said she didn't want their money hung up and started
crying Charleen's father had been an important general in
the last war after they won the war he had retired and
become a director of a multinational conglomerate but in
fact he was still a general in one of the undercover
international intelligence agencies so that for security
reasons his daughter was always covered by an agent who
tapped the phone bugged the apartment and intervened if
necessary

sometimes he would be waiting for them in a black car on a rainy night after the busses had stopped running and they couldn't find a cab offering them a ride which they always turned down sometimes they would notice a quiet man in a quiet suit across the room at a gallery opening and know it was him although he was always different sometimes he would appear leaning against a tree near the kiosk in Reese Park staring up at the branches doing nothing exerting his power his presence his control applying the pressure of the multinational financial conglomerate office in charge of the new conditions to a union it felt was too risky and counter to the mandates of intelligence intervening to destabilize it and bring it down so that they were constantly reminded if they had any ideas about retreating into silence exile cunning that they too were part of the general situation he decided to sit down and talk about everything with Charleen but of course Charleen didn't know how to talk about anything she was a stunning example of the verbal hole first of all she didn't like to talk about anything until she consulted her astrologer she had a local astrologer who followed her around all the time there were many on the island on the island astrology was more important than Christianity and then she seemed to take any analytical statement as a challenge or even an insult so that for example if he said don't you think it's fair if you see other people I see other people she would snap I'm not interested in bargaining with you see whoever you want but he would say you get angry when I see whoever I want silence he would feel as if he had fallen into a gaping hole into that nothing on the other side of something death sleep shadows phantoms ambiguities contraditions paradoxes uncertainties the maybe in her yesno system

the island's highest mountain was called Mt. Medwick
it was high enough to have
snow in the winter and had a
good steep downhill slope in
summer the main attractions
were the waterfall and the
view the view was really a
multiple of views as you went
up and around the mountain
there was no one place from
which you could see the whole
island but you could get a
kind of collage overview of
the whole thing from one
viewpoint to the next the
waterfall was spectacularly
high so that the water as it
went over the brink and down
its long free fall fell into
chunks and irregular masses
of grey of green of white of
silver of rainbow spray until it
was caught and channeled in
its chute at the distant bottom in a narrow sluice with
amazing speed one day they
all rented a car it was time to
get out of the city to get a
little perspective they brought
food and wine and drove to
the mountain on Howie Schultz
Highway for the day starting
at dawn Carl and Charleen
stayed up all night to do it
because they knew they'd

never get up at dawn so did Veronica and Victor Tony and Drecker were the only ones used to getting up in the morning Drecker was driver Tony was the only other person awake as they drove through the countryside toward Mt. Medwick Carl was able to afford the car because he had taken the job writing reports he had gone to see Bennett the exile Bennett looked like a seal very slick and streamlined and spoke with a very weird accent from having been on the island so long a speech neither island nor native but something new and unearthly like a computer taught to speak by a panel of international cyberneticists let me explain said Bennett you know nothing about maternity good but what is maternity maternity is making something out of nothing now you as a scientist engaged in research are involved in essentially the same kind of activity is it not and furthermore what is a report a report is a bureaucrat's way of making nothing of something now we have a situation here of demographic growth heading

44

toward disastrous overpopu-
lation with at the same time
high infant mortality aggravated because the land can
no longer support the growing population which moves
into the city at a rapid rate
where there are no facilities
jobs or housing but on the
other hand attempts at population control lead to charges
of oppression and genocide
therefore nothing can be done
it is how do you say it a blind
alley no way out when there
is nothing to be done what
you do is write a report and
that is why you are writing a
report to make something of
nothing in order to make
nothing of something though
undoubtedly at a higher level
of information and that is
indeed our task as savants to
struggle relentlessly to elevate
the level of information it
changes nothing but it is an
end in itself in the end it is
our substitute for god if you
know of any other end please
let me know Drecker was
trying to explain to Tony his
idea of units you see he said
everything has to be measured it doesn't matter how
it's measured as long as it's

measured measure is the mark
of a man if you see what I mean
said Drecker I'm with you so
far said Tony okay said Drecker
so my idea of units is a way of
applying measure to things we
haven't even thought of meas-
uring before like love affairs
like history like feelings like all
our little every day experiences
for example mathematicians
have recently found a way to
measure irregular catastroph-
ic events do you see what I
mean said Drecker I don't
see a goddam thing said Tony
the windmills the sheep the
deserted farmhouses and
barns fled by like migrating
birds as the car sped down
the straight empty two lane
highway there was absolutely nothing in the left hand
lane the road was smooth as
a blackboard they could have
been standing still and the
scenery moving on millions
of tiny wheels what difference
thought Drecker with two jets
flying 600 mph in the same
direction you have the impression neither is moving
standing still is a form of
movement Drecker told Tony
tell that to the boys on the
assembly line said Tony but

Drecker had his mind on
vague blocks of matter e-
merging diverging converging
they were starting to go up
the mountain the road as-
cending descending coiling
back on itself the three in the
back seat began to wake up
oh shit where are we said
Charleen I never know where
you're at said Tony that's right
cowboy said Charleen go back
to sleep Carl said next to her
she snuggled up to him she's
at her best when she's waking up he thought or going to
sleep Victor between Tony
and Drecker in the front seat
woke up with a jerk said
invisible insane went back to
sleep Carl lit a cigarette and
threw the rest of the pack out
the window he was trying to
stop smoking as they climbed
the mountain he started to
think about the upcoming
decline the upcoming decline
was at the bottom of the new
conditions along with the revolution of rising expectations when rising expectations hit the upcoming decline hell was going to break
loose it was already starting
to break loose the mountain
was full of unemployed doc-

tors of philosophy living in the woods and getting into witchcraft and astrology and who were responsible for the growth of the new cult of achronicianity an astrology based religion which rejected the notion of time for that of distance yesterday was not a different time you were in a different place everything was happening at the same time but in different places they did not believe in emotion they believed in location where are you at they would ask ideally you were centered when they asked you about yourself they would say what are your coordinates instead of holy writ they had maps and charts they taught their children not to read or write but to draw and act out reading and writing were considered forms of repression deviations from the oral tradition bulwarks of capitalism the children watched television and made origami everyone was more or less aware of the upcoming decline yet expectations continued to rise causing a loss of direction in high places which resorted increasingly to low methods producing a lapse of confidence provoking a flight of capital hastening decline stimulating official optimism raising expectations increasing contradictions Tony rolled a joint and passed it around Drecker turned the radio on and got Charlie Mingus doing Eat That Chicken which woke everybody up and got them hungry Veronica started passing around pieces of chicken and Tony opened a bottle of wine the car humming along the joint going around the bottle going around the chicken going around and bread and pâté and bananas and oranges getting high chattering laughing good music on the radio the local radio played mostly jazz and rock plus the island songs which were also very good especially to dance to the lyrics were all about revolution but the rhythms went right to the hips and groin they were all right in the car driving up the mountain direction purpose destination the destination wasn't important the important thing was to keep moving Carl knew stasis waits like a gaping hole

at the peak in Medwick Park
they peered over a precipice
the famous view the tiny city
and beyond the engulfing sea
peaceful and glistening in the
sun but vast out of scale
threatening by the pure extent of it appending a note of
pathos to their questionable
paradise and Carl saw in his
mind the fountain in Ferrell
Anderson Place representing
the expulsion from Eden which
had always seemed to him so
anachronistic in the perfect
afternoons they had eaten all
their food in the car but they
had several bottles of wine
they opened and sat around
the wooden table in the thin
air the sun warmed them but
it was chill in the shadows
Victor and Charleen were
getting along unusually well
Victor was telling her about
his latest money making
scheme relief maps for blind
tourists Charleen was derisive but not insulting almost
good humored in fact obviously high Charleen would
never have been able to get
away with the things she got
away with if she weren't so
beautiful though she wasn't
getting away with so many of

them lately people were getting to know her her reputation was catching up with her and she was visibly aging you could tell that soon it was going to be a long desperate race between cellulite and silicone when he wasn't angry with her these days Carl was feeling sorry for her except when she was waking up or falling asleep when he still could love her Veronica and Drecker were still high and coasting obviously getting it together again they went for a walk to the woods down below timberline Tony on the other hand was getting grouchy and so was Carl he was getting that soggy feeling from too much bad wine leading to one of those awful same day hangovers the thin air was making it worse lack of oxygen ten steps and he started breathing hard there were still patches of snow on the north side of boulders but the small intense spring flowers were coming up orange azure yellow the sky was luminous blue but he knew clouds could mass quickly over the mountain lowering curtains of heavy snow he felt ill at ease there were few others up here at this season the park was officially closed signs warned of uncertain weather and cautioned about the risks of exposure of losing one's way remember the signs said the mountains don't care they tallied the number of people who had died or disappeared on the various trails this year beware they said of possible abrupt and violent modifications Tony was looking surly and bored he got his transistor radio from the car and tuned in some country music oh christ said Charleen something wrong said Tony we didn't come up here to listen to your cheap gadget said Charleen look this thing set me back close to nine hundred balls and it comes with the right to listen to it said Tony are you always counting your balls she said I know how many I got he said I didn't ask how many you have are you worried about it she said lady I don't need your shit he said what makes you think I'm concerned about what you need she said wo-men like you ought to be whipped every morning he

said that's always the answer
for your type she said I don't
have a type he said I would
say it's rather common she
said you must have some-
thing real nasty up your ass
he said how boring she said
you're mean as a rabid bat he
said does that indicate you're
angry I realize you find articulation difficult perhaps you
need a little help she said I
know what you need he said
take a ride cowboy she said
I'm thinking about it he said
Victor asked if anybody wanted to hike Carl went off with
Victor Tony and Charleen still
arguing when they got back
the radio was off Tony and
Charleen were very quiet
good he thought soon everybody will have slept with everybody maybe then they'd
be like a big family maybe
that was the only kind of
family possible under the new
conditions sisters and broth-
ers in communal incest on
the other side of jealousy or
maybe they should all just
register for mates with the
government bureau of mar-
riages the marriage bureau
was a highly successful social
experiment that matched men

and women on the basis of cumputerized genetic calculations designed to produce successful offspring its escalating popularity was the consequence of claims by satisfied users that sympathetic genes produced satisfying relationships whose relative longevity was confirmed by statistics that encouraged neodarwinians some said it was merely a new form of the marriage of property taking progeny as property the fact is in many cases it gave a basis to matrimonial coupling that no other tendency could even begin to claim and provided the data for a school of erotic realists who were proponents of what they called unromantic love which however differed radically from the policies of the bureau of marriages in denying the necessity of matrimony whereas the bureau insisted on the marriage of the matching couple sight unseen claiming the importance of a social matrix while the realists objected that an imposed matrix was meretricious deleterious and an invasion of civil liberties and that furthermore

54

the government's enforced traditionalism based on an absolutely Hallmark sensibility including kitsch ceremony shoes rice and elaborate honeymoons only served to sentimentalize and remystify the essentially gutbucket nature of the relation though as many observers pointed out that was probably the government's motive as an institution since institutions needed their mystiques and mystiques needed their institutions and institutions needed their pet projects to which they could point in order to downgrade the upcoming decline by demonstrating a steady rise in the quality of life meanwhile fat slow flakes of snow were drifting down like little parachutes and Veronica and Drecker had not returned soon the contours of the ground were covered with a smooth white sheet they decided to split into two parties Tony and Victor would wait while Carl and Charleen would look they slid down among the boulders toward tree line it wasn't that he was jealous it was that now she was going to be dreamy and moony about Tony for the next several weeks until she got bored with it he was waiting to hear about the virtues of the proletariat the rude strengths of the workingman maybe she would even go so far as to get a job that would be nice they would probably be eating spaghetti every night what's wrong with you said Charleen as they skidded among the boulders nothing he said you look jealous she said about what he said you have no right to ask me that she said I'm not jealous he said yes you are she said it doesn't compromise you she said that's just your own cheap reaction she said you're incredibly middle class she said it's going to become a factor with Tony that's all he said too bad the boys won't be able to hang out together on the street corner anymore she said I told you I don't care what you do as long as it doesn't become a factor he said with you everything becomes a factor I think you want factors maybe you want to sleep with Tony maybe that's a factor boys will be boys I'm tired of your factors

I can make love with people
without it becoming a factor
she said isn't it pretty to think
so he said meanwhile they
had forgotten to look for Veronica and Drecker it was starting to get dark the wind was
rising the snow was heavier it
was noticeably colder let's go
back I don't see them anywhere he said okay she said
where are you going he said
it's this way he said are you
going to start another argument she said you know you
have no sense of direction he
said I've never known anybody who was so consistent-
ly wrong about everything
she said I've never known
anybody who was so consist-
ently never wrong about anything he said it was getting
quite cold they were dressed
in light clothing they were
standing in the middle of a
blank white space their foot-
prints were covered over almost as soon as they made
them visibility whited out at
about ten feet it was like
nowhere it was like walking
into nothing look this is the
reality principle let's be serious he said I miss my children she said

Charleen felt like a gaping hole a hoard of lacks amorphous a negative that had never been developed a lax often lux now dull null sitting uncomfortably between Carl and Tony as Drecker drove them down out of the snow nobody talking the car was like a vacuum even Veronica and Drecker seemed emptied who has a cigarette asked Carl I thought you stopped said Veronica pulling out her pack I did he said he lit his cigarette Charleen found it depressing for some reason that he couldn't stop smoking in fact she was depressed maybe she was getting her period maybe she was depressed because she was getting her period she always forgot she got depressed when she was getting her period she always forgot she was getting her period maybe that was because she was a right brain person she knew she was a right brain person because she was left handed she thought maybe Tony was a right brain person even though he was right handed he made love in a left handed way it was very nice crouching on the picnic table maybe it was because he was Italian the Italians seemed like a right brain race she couldn't remember if she'd ever slept with an Italian before though she'd always liked Italy Tony had never been to Italy Carl was definitely a left brain person very articulate but clumsy she couldn't stand the way he peeled potatoes part of the attraction she had felt for Carl was because they were opposites now it was part of the revulsion Drecker was also left brain but making love with him on the boat made it somehow right brain like he was crude in his approach he enjoyed doing things to her in public it was a form of humiliation she could get into humiliation but she couldn't get into beating like the time she let Drecker spank her with a ping pong paddle it turned her off but he was very nice when he finally got down to it it was thick and kind of wedgey as opposed to Carl who was long and thin Tony was very full and moved nicely it was kind of delicate actually Victor was different all the time that was Victor's problem he couldn't make up his mind whether he was left brain or right brain for one thing it was interesting making love with a lot of men making love with a lot of men made her feel like a man for some reason it also made her feel very feminine very passive she liked that feeling of giving in giving up it really turned her on it was very sensuous it made her feel very female very aggressive almost acquisitive she felt as if she were exploiting them it was always a strain making choices this or that yes or no it never made any sense to her she worked by analogy not dichotomy she would have made a good actress or maybe playwright Drecker worked by dichotomy there was something phallic about dichotomy dichotomy was schizoid by nature if this exists that doesn't yes or no analogy was maybe was feminine was inclusive but it was solipsistic subject to delusion actually she also worked by dichotomy it depended it depended on what was happening on what was around her she was defined by what was around her that seemed

like a sensible way of going
about things otherwise you
got out of contact though it
also got her into trouble since
she tended to get completely
into a situation and then completely forgot about other sit-
uations she was also com-
pletely into even though they
might be totally in conflict it
was amazing how well she
knew herself and how little it
mattered as soon as she got
into a situation where it mattered it went completely out
of her mind that is he used to
be very articulate she wondered what had happened to
Carl he'd become completely sullen and surly never
talked except to contradict
her she didn't see any reason
she had to put up with that
oh well in a world of endless
possibility the grass is always
greener despite every catastrophe her expectations kept
rising Drecker was driving
fast too fast they were down
out of the snow now he was
in a hurry to get down to The
Reiser before sunset so he
could see the quote postcard
run by the post office once a
week during tourist season at
ebb tide just before sunset

the post office would truck all the postcards mailed by the tourists down to The Reiser and dump them in the ocean and Drecker always took childish pleasure in watching the dry but colorful cascade pour out of the trucks into the water this was officially called the quote postcard run which the post office justified by saying maybe some of them will get there anyway in any case word had gotten around about what the post office was doing and the postcard run had itself become a big tourist attraction in fact there were now many postcards of it and if during tourist season by any chance there weren't enough postcards for the postcard run the television stations would buy expensive quantities of cards for the post office to dump rather than lose their hottest feature story to the great relief of the merchants around The Reiser who stood to lose thousands of balls worth of perishables purchased to sell to the crowds who came to watch the run at the food stands and cafes and in fact the television stations were secretly subsidized by the government tourist agency because the postcard run had become worth its weight in balls to the economy of the island as international tourist publicity demonstrating the quaint native customs as well as the lengths the islanders would go to please tourists she herself was eager to get down because she had an appointment with someone from the quote escort service that was actually Carl's idea but she certainly wasn't going to tell him about it information is power and anyway it was none of his business but she was curious she'd never done anything like that before she wanted to see what that was all about and she certainly needed the balls so she could get out of this place also she was supposed to meet Drecker down at Ramazotti Bay tonight she wondered if Drecker would be in the mood she watched Veronica in the front seat pressed close to Drecker she knew she had funny feelings about Veronica she wondered whether it was because of

Drecker or because of Carl
she wondered what it was
like for Veronica with Drecker
and with Carl she wondered
what it was like for Drecker
and Carl with Veronica she
was tired maybe it was because of getting lost in the
snow or maybe it was be-
cause of her period or maybe
she was tired of all these
complicated relations she had
really been in love with Carl
where had that all gone why
was it so boring actually
Drecker was getting boring
too this was getting to seem
less and less like a world of
endless possibility the thought
occured to her that maybe
endless possibility was impossible but then she believed in
the impossible the impossible was just the other side of
the possible when the possible became impossible as it
so often seemed to be then
the impossible became possible like when something
becomes nothing you make
of nothing something it happened to her again and again
the way pleasure seemed to
consume itself and turn into
the opposite and then she
panicked and started grop-

ing for pleasure again not so much for pleasure itself as to avoid the gaping hole waiting were she to admit the whole thing was impossible the fatal fall into final loneliness the death of desire itself therefore she desired only what she couldn't have because if she had it she knew it wasn't worth it and when she asked herself if this wasn't crazy the best answer she could give was yes and no she knew it was necessary to choose and she chose her contradictions which she couldn't contain but maybe one day they were approaching Basinski Bridge over The Rosen River into the city they could see the tall office buildings in the middle of the town and further down the tower of The Campanella near Ferrell Anderson Place as she filed through the patterns of her passions in both senses of the word which after demystification amounted to the thought that all patterns are painful repetitions as well as pleasurable reduplications how well she thought as they went over the bridge watching the bright sails bobbing in the river and The Campanella whose bells she could now faintly hear singing in the sun over Oldtown all that matched the rhythms of the island itself with its happiness fetish its evasion of the fact of death even the hidden crematoria the scattering of ashes in the sea by state disposal units the gay native wakes which were such profitable tourist attractions indeed the happiness fetish had its sinister side those insistent evasions without which that famous sweet to do nothing tone of the islanders could not be sustained like the way nobody did anything about the epidemic of rabid bats that came out at evening swooping around the citizens chattering in the outdoor cafes and the corruption which everybody took for granted and that nevertheless eroded confidence in all civic functions and was even starting to eat away the texture of social life sports fans have no faith in government today's headline read survey shows distrust of large groups who has a cigarette said Carl what's the matter you nervous Char-

leen said he glared at her
Tony pulled out a pack of the
harsh native brand and offered one to Carl without
looking at him she asked
Drecker to drop her off at
Stanky and Cox what are you
doing down at Stanky and
Cox Carl asked suspiciously
Stanky Street was the escort
district and he happened to
know that the offices of the
state escort service were on
Cox Avenue it's none of your
affair I have an appointment
she said they were caught in
a traffic jam on Owen Road
Drecker turned on the radio
and got a bulletin that achronician terrorists had stuffed a
bank with cotton nothing
could be done all transac-
tions were blocked the fire
department's special chronic
emergency squad had sur-
rounded the bank blocking
Rojeck causing a huge traffic
jam on Owen Road as far as
Branca Parkway the achronicians specialized in stunts that
wasted time threw off sched-
ules and generally gummed
up the forces of efficiency
and progress that were in-
vading the island always leaving their stop time slogans on

the walls like time is the tool
of capitalist exploitation I'm
going to be late for work said
Veronica Veronica had a new
job she was now working at
The Same Thing her job was
sitting at a table during slack
hours and pretending she was
having a good time to lure
customers in off the street it
was easy work but she didn't
enjoy it Drecker changed the
station and got one of the
island songs

> revolution
> stop pollution
> lazy folk
> always broke
> got no need
> to be freed
> mister sorrow
> come tomorrow
> ain't no crime
> wastin time
> play the game
> get the blame
> empty table
> make you able
> got no food
> gettin screwed
> got no balls
> poor man crawls
> revolution
> stop pollution

Carl asked Tony if he wanted
to drop off at The Tartine to

get something to eat Tony
looked away vaguely said he
had an appointment at The
Smiling Lemming Charleen
was already becoming a factor actually she sort of enjoyed being a factor though
she didn't like to admit it it
made her feel she existed at
times when she wasn't exactly sure she existed I'm loved
therefore I exist how well she
knew herself how little good
it did her she wondered what
it was going to be like when
her seven lovers came or was
it eight depending on whether she should count wo-
men she didn't think so that
was different it would probably be like it was before a
little like Snow White and the
Seven Dwarfs none were e-
nough to give her everything
she wanted but each added
something brought out a different part of herself it made
her feel male exploitative co-
lonial rapacious it was also
like being torn to pieces everybody got a piece but that
was sexy too bacchic it made
her a little crazy she wanted
to be torn to pieces and she
wanted to be put together
she had thought maybe Carl

could put her together but
maybe once you're torn to
pieces you can't be put back
together maybe it was be-
cause of what Carl called the
great shift Carl had the idea
they were living through the
breakup of one cultural amalgam in transition to another
cultural amalgam the new cultural amalgam was flux also
known as the new conditions
maybe she was going into a
state of permanent flux what
she needed was a profession
something to define her that
was one of the reasons she
admired Veronica so much
Veronica was tired of being
defined by men she always
had some kind of profession
it wasn't only making money
Drecker had offered to support her but she didn't want
it she wanted to do it herself
her current profession was
sitting and enjoying herself
she thought that was a pretty
good profession even though
Veronica didn't enjoy it maybe that was why women were
going in for men's styles on
the island this year because
men had a better deal oh well
in a world of endless possibility the grass is always greener or at least stronger she

would have to consult her astrologer about the escort service maybe she could make a profession of the escort service anyway she certainly needed the balls she would have to talk to Veronica who was now at The Same Thing on Wyatt where she had walked with Carl at a table pretending she was enjoying herself she had the feeling she had to keep going or she would fall in to what she didn't stop to ask but sat there smiling gaily at Carl who was telling her about his maternity report for which he already had big plans he said that maternity was the key to the new conditions in that the new conditions called for fraternity as opposed to paternity or the authority of seniority while sorority and fraternity were favored by maternity Veronica laughed gaily too much she said ah but you see that's exactly the problem said Carl limits are necessary but undesirable therefore we substitute measure for limit to monitor the infinite but measure is repetition which is nothing an echo but then nothing plus something equals everything

so measure equals pleasure
and progressively cancels the
crime of time in the maternity of eternity until we reach
the primal rhyme om-mom
ecco echo

Victor of course knew that Charleen didn't want him
around and suspected that the pains in his chest were no
coincidence he believed that she had weird powers and
that she was using them to get him off the island and out of
her life other things had been happening he reflected as
he sat shivering in his tiny bare room trying to massage his
chest like the pillow first the pillow case had disappeared
and then a few days later the pillow itself nowhere it could
have gone no one else could get into his room as if she
were trying to make it so uncomfortable for him he would
finally be forced to move he wouldn't go so far as to say she
had a little doll of him with a pin stuck through it though he
wouldn't put it past her astrologer friends not to mention
the achronicians she knew and today finally one of his two
towels was gone through the gaping hole what next

what next what next Victor predicted that more and more would disappear through the gaping hole faster and faster till people learned how to control the hole to go through it and find out what was on the other side the only way to find out what was on the other side was through prediction and the medium of prediction was the written word there the achronicians were correct the written word coexists coexists with what coexists with the written word all written words comprise a vast and growing coincidence extending into past and future doubling and redoubling complex reflections not so with spoken words which disappear into the air into the ear into the gaping hole even the written word of history emerges at the fine edge of the future prediction of the past the word written only for the future never the moment telling the way was and is will be the written world pregnant with prophecy all mirrored in its mutations and permutations semiology recapitulates biology our grammar is our drama our syntax our sin tax our fictions our predictions change the word and change the world or so quipped Victor delirious in his tiny room also known on The Walker as Schizzy Vic caught in the ongoing flow of the ongoing flow no way out but straight ahead Tony felt wonderful it had started when he started fucking a girl from the office at the factory he didn't especially like her and he didn't especially like fucking her but one night they were drinking and he figured what the hell they were drinking her name was Lola she was a native also he was tired of being alone late at night with his bottle of whisky next thing he knew he was also sleeping with a girl he met in The Tartine he didn't even remember how he met her then it was that sweet bitch on the mountain he

thought she hated his guts but she really wanted him and

this was after months of unwanted celibacy one after
another it was funny how those things clumped he'd had a
clump like that last year he'd had five of them on the string
the way it always happened he'd start concentrating on one
of them and the others would drift away then he'd break
up with that one and he'd be celibate again wondering
what the point of it all was supposed to be it was funny the
way he really felt good tonight when he hadn't slept or
anything after waking up this morning feeling really
dragged and tired out like too much smoking and drinking
and fucking he'd felt like he didn't even want to see
another woman for a month and now his body felt alive
and solid and horny he felt like he was walking around on
top of an animal in prime condition really tuned and now

he was going over to The Same Thing to see Veronica and
he knew he was going to fuck Veronica tonight it was a
sure thing if this kept up he probably should start going to
the track he stopped to buy a lottery ticket he felt like he
was caught up in some kind of flow all he had to do was
keep himself from thinking about it if he started thinking
about it too much it would screw it up the thing to do was
just keep riding the edge of it not try to get ahead of it by

thinking about it or by pushing it or not let it pass him by but just keep riding what was happening like a wave though right now it felt so strong he knew he could think about it or push it or let it go and catch up with it or do all sorts of tricks with it and it wouldn't make any difference he just didn't want any static from Carl he knew Carl could bring him down it wasn't so much that

Carl was thinking about everything all the time it was that he was thinking about everything in the wrong way it was like his thinking wasn't part of his doing it wasn't the way Tony was thinking the way Tony was thinking was not about what he was doing when he was thinking it was what he was doing he was doing thinking not thinking doing or to put it another way his doing was like a form of thinking like when he was talking it was like he was thinking out loud it was part of his thinking he just happened to be talking or like if he was fucking it was a way of talking that was a way of thinking that was a way of doing and the doing was not something he did but like he always knew what he was going to do and he was just following what was happening and he always knew what was going to happen this had happened to him before this had happened to him before and when it stopped happening he had no idea what had happened or how or why it had stopped the whole thing just went completely out of his mind he didn't even remember it had happened he only remembered it when it was happening like when it wasn't happening it slipped into a gaping hole and when it was happening it wasn't like he was remembering but like remembering was happening happening happening was what it was all about walking down Wyatt he saw Carl coming out of The Same Thing and head the other way as Tony went in he noticed that the shape of the island on a map they had hanging up looked just like a giant oyster he stopped to examine the shape of the city itself with its web of streets in Oldtown wondering why it made him think of the past of his childhood living in the city was like living in the past and present at the same time it was like living in your own head but at the same time not maybe that was the attraction of the city exactly that it was not nature but like the record of a collective head a mass fingerprint Veronica was not having a good time having a good time she looked like she was having a good time because that was her job but she was not really there even though she was there it was the same thing when she tried the escort service on a part time basis and kept dreaming of worms cut in half but it just goes to show she reflected that the escort service is no different from other jobs you're there and you're not there part of you says yes and part of you says no and if you start getting into maybe or even worse suppose forget it it's a disaster that's why all jobs stink and it wasn't much different with school personally she liked to get into suppose but then she'd always been a dreamer she was not a yesno person suppose for example Bennett were not such a yesno person sometimes she still missed Bennett suppose she had tried harder to accommodate to Bennett there might have been some basis maybe she could have found a way of relating to Bennett as an onoff person because while she wasn't a yesno person she was an onoff person the trouble was while Bennett was definitely a yesno person he was definitely not an onoff person he was always on compared to Victor who was always off or Carl who was always half on half off while she herself was either on or off but never in between but maybe there was some way of correlating yesno with onoff yes with on and no with off the thing is yes means choice while on means not choosing the same

thing with no off no off didn't make any sense in fact it meant the opposite of what it said it meant on on the other hand on was no backwards and in fact when Bennett said no it turned her on and when he said yes it turned her off no wonder they didn't get along they were too much alike but like mirror images she was like Bennett but backwards

80

which explained why they turned one another on at the same time they turned one another off well that was a relief but still sometimes she still missed Bennett there might have been some basis suppose she had turned herself off permanently to balance his on or maybe learned to be on all the time or maybe to say yes when he said yes and no when he said no the thing is while two no's make a yes two yesses don't

make a no so she would get stuck in yes while he went back to no and they'd be in the same place again the hell with it she thought smiling gaily out the big plate glass window of The Same Thing she was definitely not enjoying herself enjoying herself but in fact that was often the case she was just doing the same thing in The Same Thing and getting paid for it that cheered her up some to the extent that at least she began to enjoy herself not enjoying herself Carl was fascinated by a phrase often used by the islanders on the other side of the wind it was usually accompanied by a broad sweep of the arm he was fascinated by it because he couldn't understand what it meant and the islanders were completely unable to explain it to him when they tried they usually ended up by shrugging their shoulders and repeating on the other side of the wind with a broad sweep of the arm

as if the meaning of the other side of the wind were on the other side of the wind the phrase had an opacity about it a complete impenetrability yet despite this or maybe because of it it was completely open not open like a window to be sure despite its transparency but open like a tunnel at either end so that one could say for example death waits for us all on the other side of the wind or the other side of the wind wears a different way and one was immediately understood and while Carl was not completely sure why he wondered if he hadn't stumbled on the secret of the way words worked and he wondered further whether if one understood the way words worked one would not understand the way oneself worked and whether that was not the kind of knowledge one could never know directly but only through using wisdom winking from the other side of the wind

82

Drecker felt like he had awakened on the other side of the
wind he felt like he had died and come back as a ghost
wandering among dead flies and the hulks of old rowboats
the remains of last night's dinner with Veronica still on the
table shrinking from contact with surfaces an inhabitant of
a parallel universe not quite in sync with this one he
thought of the sloop slapping in its slip and of calling off his
appointments for the morning of the sails flapping into the
wind and booming out as he came about toward the high
sea for absolutely nowhere where he belonged it was a
strange feeling he became aware of this morning not a new
feeling but a strange one that had been inside him growing
and that he had just this morning started to recognize
when he got out of bed Veronica already gone looked at
the overflowing ash trays and the empty glasses and said
hello to it for the first time as every man he

supposed must one day that basically his life was over that is that it would go on but that nothing now would change that he was on the other side of something of himself that units for him were no longer emerging but receding into the stale chiaroscuro of grey mornings and lonely fucks knowing how little one is oneself how much one's fate is mated with the world knowing why one does what one does but doing it the self in mourning watching the progress of its ghost better to set sail into nothingness than enter the quiet companionship of people waiting to die he would wash his ghost this morning and dress it and polish its shoes and send it out into the world with instructions to be nice to everybody maybe people would be kind to it in return pet it give it dinner make love to it and pay it compliments gorge it with life so that by the end of the evening he might even be fond of it again

the weather was bad people were coming out of the bush into the city to shake themselves in front of the fires in the bars like wet dogs sometimes in fact they brought wet dogs with them dogs they had to wet down first with lawn hoses to get the desired wet dog effect since bad weather for the islanders accustomed to blue sky and balmy temperature would have been hardly noticed elsewhere but here for example you would ask someone if they wanted to go to a movie and they would say are you kidding it's drizzling out but nevertheless the so-called wet dog effect so affected by the islanders and respected even by those who thought it recherché brought out something about the islanders which foreigners ridiculed but Charleen admired for the wet dog effect was an affectation of men not of dogs

and was an effective manner of expressing a kind of floating discontent not merely with the weather or rather not with the weather at all since there were spontaneous outbreaks of wet dog in the city on the sunniest days people all over town standing in front of fires and shaking themselves and not necessarily in front of fires either and when this happened it would hit the headlines which would proclaim a wet dog day with exclamation points and there would be shots of people shaking themselves on the evening news and at this point the government would take notice because revolutions on the island were invariably preceded by wet dog attacks and you could be sure the president would be on television later that same evening shaking himself like a wet dog and giving a fireside chat foreigners found this manner of conducting politics outrageous

but she found it edifying and wished that politics back home were conducted in a similar way it was what was known here as expressive politics of course there were polls and votes but the islanders considered it lunatic to institute a government or a policy on the basis of numbers since obviously three or four people for or against something in a casual way were worth less than one person who was passionate about the thing now she considered what after all was government all about in the long view in the long view government was an institution that was supposed to augment felicity now how did you know if a government was augmenting felicity or not unless you knew whether citizens were happy or unhappy lethargic or enthusiastic angry or swooning with contentment the wet dog effect was a measure of such things crude but in its way accurate

actually she knew that Bennett was currently working on a report about how the wet dog effect could be rationalized and handled by computers and why not after all feelings were information too she also knew that Bennett by the way was very angry at Carl because of the way his maternity report was turning out the report was turning out to be against maternity but for paternity a point of view obviously difficult to justify but which didn't surprise her in the least given Carl's basic hostility toward women she always knew that underneath Carl's sulking dependence on her and his adolescent scenes of rebellion which echoed as far as she could tell his similar filial relations with his wife who he had left on the mainland lay a layer of contempt which the trouble was she felt might be justified but that was still no excuse for his feeling that way because she knew very well the ways in which she was contemptible she had been through three kinds of psychotherapy yes she had changed so what she had improved herself three different times in three different ways so what she still felt the dark undertow into the nameless abyss after the path of excess after the path of moderation after the way of the body after the way of the mind nothing was ever enough the god of unlimited expectations was the same as the god of the nameless abyss there was something between everything and nothing she could never seem to grasp that lacked substance for her that very something the islanders with their complicated and pointless system of rituals and customs seemed so content with was exactly what she had no talent for the ordinary was not her cup of tea her talent was for the extraordinary

but the extraordinary seemed to lead right back to the nameless abyss she was trying to escape like the time she found the perfect lover and entered a state of sustained ecstasy pleasure bondage do with me what you will she would have let him kill her if he wanted to in fact she sometimes wanted him to and there it was she felt it had something to do with the last war the last war had destroyed something immaterial that was even more disastrous than all its material destruction which was enormous it had destroyed belief not belief in this or that but belief in itself so that now caught between the banal credulity of the islanders and the facile nihilism of her own speedy set which were only the heads or tails of the new conditions more and more people like herself felt the need to weave their own web from the loose ends of the international yesno system a tissue a texture a synthetic a fabrication of maybes

ennervated stasis   irretrievable loss   insubstantial depravity   emotional deprivation   energy leak   time drift   night sweats   quick lays   cheap tricks   terminal cruelties   abominable maledic-tions   lost convictions   ephemeral phenomena   hollow voices   phantasmal degradations   sha-ky nerves   degenerated generation   wasted se-men   bad dreams   wrecked relations
depress-ing speleology of consciousness   detestable musi-cians of desire   devastations of spindrift hope   ne-

oindustrial data calibrate spittoons   persistence of dis-
organized actualities   augmentations of the indefinite
        irresistible charisma of tangibility   impalpable
conclusions diminish vitality   demented synapses double hullabaloo   pitiful evidence provokes postulations
        insensate professors negate incertitudes   enig-
matic verifications blitz mysterious   callow theories
trivialize dreams   ponderous dessications dismember
stupendous   citations tend to support   debriefing
of cosmos proceeds   stupor afflicts the boondocks
        and yet the possibilities   despite the starving
slums   an island so blue-green   so round and
inclusive
                if you could believe the peasants' opti-
mism   credulous as a peasant was island jive   there
was no peasant class as such   farms depopulated by
agribusiness run by computer   a neoindustrial peas-
antry created by the state   a crude optimism rein-
forced by the media   pessimists were ostracized ridiculed lost their jobs   peasant syndicates pushed bro-
therhood solid aridity forever   but the smallest frus-
trations unleashed snarling discontent   therefore contact with reality was strictly prohibited   each hovel had
its TV stereo console   the Secretary for Happiness was
constantly hysterical   polls indicate depression in south
send circus   tactical squads of comedians on constant
alert   peasant gurus appeared preaching a resigned
optimism   deposed foreign spiritual leaders arrived
en masse   wisdom found easy pickings in hard times
        intellectuals dropouts and nouveaux riches discov-
ered religion   any religion if it wasn't your own
        meanwhile ugly rumors persisted about the po-
lice   sinister undercurrents concerning multinational
corporate intelligence superpowers   the will to believe became public relations   shoe laces and love
affairs were computerized   it was all part of the
process   ideas and thought became information and
process   it was the process that really mattered   phi-

losophers were videotaped working in their studies   people were edified by watching them think   action
painting essentialized pure action no painting   everybody tried to improve and got worse   but the effort
counted it was sincere   dealers in good will were
getting rich   they incorporated as nonprofit with government grants   people changed so fast they were
unrecognizable   the whole culture was an ongoing
improvisation   even multinational intelligence superpowers were losing track   hijackings proliferated slogans appeared on city walls   Mary's apologies and a
plane to Cuba   liberate prisoners imprisoned for writing on walls   the government created a department of
prognostication   Bennett wrote a report on the unpredictable   sanity appeared futile so madness became
chic   yet something was happening despite apparent
foolishness   big time financial maneuvers requiring
demographic manipulation   orders came down to the
mass media   support dropouts critics mystics counter
culture crazies   rasputins of the marginal suddenly got
lucky   culture gangs formed flourished fought and
failed   power shifts were shaking the establishment
monolith   international behemoths locked in silent
invisible struggle   conflicting ideologies created an
interminable terminal babble   the authorities panicked
and lost their grip   the civil service was grouchy and
nervous   Charleen found the chaos fruitful if scary
     people's patterns were evident and evidently de-
structive   consequences of liberation proved discouraging but exhilarating   personal relations were definitely shot to hell   all right maybe they needed to
be   she certainly needed to break with Carl   and
with Drecker and even with Tony   who she had hardly
gotten together with   it was the time of the assas-
sins   everything was breaking up and going to pieces
     the hell with it let it go   only Victor was getting it
together suddenly   he had come out of the clo-

set   and walked right into Bennett's waiting arms
she would have to talk to Veronica   when hus-
bands become lovers wives become friends
                                                                    being
fucked up the ass made her think about the meaning of life
Veronica said it was a cul de sac death a violation of her
interior space   against this what every time Drecker
did it to her the question came up not as a question as a
reflex of despair why did she let him   basically she
didn't like Drecker Drecker treated her like a piece of shit
something about her liked being treated like a piece of shit
that's why she liked him   that's why she let him the
question was there it didn't need to be asked it was there
and she wanted to face it as part of herself   she wanted
to face it but when she faced it she didn't know what to do
with it it was a painful standoff so painful she would rather
evade it   that's why it was good to talk to another
woman finally when she tried to talk to a man about being
fucked in the ass she got funny vibes   it was always
taken as a come on she could see Charleen was taking her
seriously and knew what she was talking about she was
thinking about it   finally Charleen said she thought
that being fucked up the ass was a dead end and that was
why it was depressing that it was a kind of exploitation   it was literally being colonized and she said this
she said even though frankly she liked being fucked in the
ass so do I so do I said Veronica   what it comes to
maybe go on said Veronica is that maybe we shouldn't let
ourselves be fucked in the ass whether we like it or
not   right on said Veronica but that doesn't answer the
question no it doesn't answer the question but maybe it's
one of those questions that have no answer   maybe
it's one of those questions whose answer is tragedy maybe
the wisdom of the bourgeoisie is in avoiding those
questions maybe we should go back to the middle
class   I've already tried going back to it said Veronica
but it isn't there anymore they all want to be like us well

then maybe we're it Charleen answered   but you
know she continued maybe it's the same for men I mean of
course it's a form of violation it's an assertion of power of
domination   but it's also fucking shit really and who
wants to fuck shit it's a consummation of garbage not only
a wasted copulation but also a copulation with waste   I
mean it's a figuration of the nameless abyss toward which
we're all drawn into which we all pass sooner or later
maybe for them it's desperation too   maybe it's like
people afraid of heights wanting to jump off of them
maybe it comes from reaching into the gaping hole
groping for something that's never there   maybe that's
when the gaping hole becomes the nameless abyss I could
never talk to Carl this way I'm glad I can talk to you so am
I   but what are we talking about asked Veronica about
the meaning of life and the thing is if it has one you don't
need to talk about it   but we need to talk about it said
Veronica because for example some times you're having a
lot of fun and everything's going fine but there's this
despair   or is that only me no right if you stand still
long enough to let things catch up with you and it's the same
thing if you fall in love   right that's the worse thing that
can happen a catastrophe every time I'm through with that
trip I mean forever though sometimes I think of having a
baby   yes once every month yes right and bringing it
up by myself find a father via russian roulette I'd rather not
know who it is I'd rather he didn't   but we know that's
not the answer maybe there is no answer yes maybe look at
it this way if there's no answer maybe there's no question
        well that's why I like Drecker's approach you know
I'm stupid and I prefer being stupid oh does he come on
with you that way too yes   he just refuses to ask those
questions yes that's right but then he fucks me up the ass
and I start thinking about the meaning of life yes   I sort
of like the way Tony comes on you know I got a hardon for
you baby at least when he says he's got one he's got
one   that's right Drecker's just pretending to be dumb

Tony really is well maybe that's the answer yes that's the answer for Tony because there's no question for him   I don't know if Tony is dumb it's just not a head thing said Veronica you like Tony Charleen asked he's lucky I like lucky men said Veronica   lucky men don't ask questions they just know what to do otherwise it's all loose ends when I get that loose end feeling it makes me very up tight   yes the best thing for loose ends is when you come together yes and the worst thing is when you don't come at all like when he comes   yes when you're looking at things from the other side of an orgasm they really look different in the escort service I was always bugged by loose ends   really yes I felt like a loose end myself really are you queer I'm queer sometimes but it's not lucky to be queer no but it's less harsh   that's right it's not lucky to be harsh either no but sometimes harsh isn't so bad it keeps you in touch and keeping in touch is lucky   when Veronica looked into Charleen's eyes she could see the fear there she didn't want to see it but she was fascinated also it frightened her a lot   Carl was angry at Charleen again this time because she laughed at him when he told her he was thinking about becoming a saint and she should too   Carl said he had thought about it and while it was complicated it was also fundamentally simple involving a decision always to do what was good and right   that's when she started laughing and he said no she shouldn't laugh he knew what she was laughing about but it was the only way to go about things   he said that he knew it was complicated to do what was good and right but that deciding to do it was a big step in the right direction   he said he was aware of the complications but that the first thing to do was to refuse to be complicated about it otherwise you simply got nowhere   he said being complicated about it was another way of being bad and wrong and avoiding the mysterious difficulty of that simple decision to be good and right   he said you had to uncomplicate yourself enough to make that simple decision he said there were a lot of people who were cynical or just utilitarian who believed pragmatism was the best way to get things done quite true   but he said it was not a way of getting the good and right things done they always got put off sometimes it was better to do nothing   he said a lot of people would tell you things were more complicated than that but that usually this was just a form of complacency it not smugness   he said it was also extremely important to remember complication could also be at bottom a sophisticated form of fear the greater the complication the greater the fear   he said the important things were basically simple and while he was not against complication if it was simply an evasion of those things it was based on fear   he said you shouldn't be discouraged if despite wanting to be good and right most things you did were bad and wrong you didn't become a saint overnight   he said it was something that happened gradually and sometimes suddenly but if it was suddenly it could be a big shock you might not survive like martyrs   he said martyrs probably brought it on themselves and it wasn't his style that you became a saint out of selfishness not altruism for your own good finally   he said if other people got something out of it so much the better that wasn't the point if that was the point forget it it wouldn't work   he finally asked what was so funny she had been giggling and chuckling the more he talked the more she laughed now she responded with great convulsive snorts   you can't be a saint she told him between snorts you're not human enough to be a saint first you've got to learn how to be human   meanwhile the island drifted along as usual with its quiet golden mornings its long happy afternoons and vivid evenings saints or no saints the gaping holes still gaped   the sound of smashing bottles could still be heard late into the night accompanied by screams and angry voices the usual teenage mob fights took their usual toll   down at Stanky and Cox the escort hotels were thriving and life proceeded as well as it could on the basis of faulty conclusions and withheld information   at Gionfriddo Hospital the surgical contraception industry drew hundreds wanting their tubes tied or vasectomies as part of the sex toy program sex change doctors were getting rich   Gionfriddo was also where scientists were working on the death vaccine to immunize people against death the idea was to administer small doses of death before the fact   the doses were gradually increased in size till when death finally came you would be immune to it the vaccinations were usually given in connection with sexual intercourse   to make it less dolorous the doctors said administered in a product called little pieces of death which when taken orally would mix with the sexual juices   this was of course still experimental and subjects were paid to try it Victor tried it when he was broke he claimed it sprained his cock and was suing   he also said that the little pieces of death he had taken had unleashed forces in him that were the cause of all of his later troubles   he was aware that many things you did unleashed forces love affairs friendships going to the store chance even spitting not to mention things like astrology tarot magic   you might even say that life was a matter of unleashing forces but he claimed that little pieces of death were especially potent especially in unleashing malign forces

      he claimed he was the victim of irreversible malign forces unleashed by the doctors   he said unleashed forces were blind and always irreversible we're all victims of them   the only thing to do with irreversible blind forces once unleashed is illuminate them   illuminated irreversible blind forces can be reversed with enough illumination through magic or art   scholars disputed whether these reversals were real or imaginary others said it didn't matter   some claimed the reversals were imaginary but the effects were real reality being imaginary   anyway Victor was doing his very best to

illuminate and reverse his unleashed forces   the one
really good thing about his unleashed forces was that they
were unleashed   unleashed forces were a source of
power he did not want to leash them   among the
peasants unleashed forces were considered very lucky it
gave their crazies status   peasant crazies were getting
hard to find they supposedly hung around The Smiling
Lemming   it was said they knew how to use their
unleashed forces without leashing them   that was what
Victor wanted feeling that was right and good for him
now   every night he hung around The Smiling Lemming
with Bennett looking for peasant crazies   Bennett and
Victor were getting along very well despite Victor's craziness and sprained cock   Bennett was good for Victor
Bennett processed all Victor's ambivalences through his
yesno system   when Victor's ambivalences were processed through Bennett's yesno system they came out as
choices   Victor was astonished a new world opened
up for him light filled his brain   sane or crazy Bennett
would say right or wrong good or bad yesno yesno
     Victor's synapses snapped to attention it was like zen
but zen turned him off   this yesno stuff turned him on
like a reversed unleashed illuminated irreversible blind
force   all his doom driven depressions took a holiday
his paradoxes went on a picnic   or speaking in the
tongue of the peasant crazies chicken likken is likken
chicken   Tony thought he must be out of shape
because he was feeling so low   it had to be from
drinking and screwing around too much in the bars
     every night he would go from The Tartine to The
Same Thing drinking beer   ending up in The Smiling
Lemming drinking schnapps and coca-cola with Carl and
Charleen   often some of the others would be there
listening to Carl and Charleen argue   if Drecker wasn't
around he went home with Veronica if Carl split with
Charleen   she and Carl could keep a nasty fight going
till three in the morning   Tony would always wait

around for Carl to split but sometimes he didn't shit   he had to get up early to work and went to sleep dreading birdchirp   Veronica was okay but if he screwed Charleen she kept him up all night   it took her an hour to come and if she didn't she got nasty   she was a good lay but a tough one then she started knocking Carl   then soon she wanted to make love again and that was only round two   after a night with her he felt much friendlier to Carl out of sympathy   not that he didn't like screwing her he just had to get up early   if he could sleep till one oclock like the others it would be okay   with a crazy life like that no wonder he was getting out of shape   but the craziness allowed him to forget how it felt to be in shape   in shape for what to wake up early for his pointless job in shape   he didn't know whether it was better being in shape or out of shape   it was the shape of his life that was out of shape was why   but he didn't like being out of shape because it made him feel unlucky   feeling unlucky made him feel low feeling low made him feel sorry for himself   feeling sorry for himself made him drink drinking made him feel out of shape   out of shape unlucky unlucky out of shape he bought himself a lottery ticket   what did Drecker have Drecker had nothing his life was like a gaping hole   Carl woke up at noon with a hangover but happy alone she wasn't there   the apartment was quiet calm a little traffic noise drifted in from the Place   he knew by tonight he'd be feeling horny and lonely but that was tonight   now as he drank his coffee he felt himself expand and fill the apartment   he breathed easy muscles relaxing out of sleep dreams still drifting through his head   he knew he'd attained the condition of the blessed it usually occurred in the morning   he decided as his first act of sainthood he would stop smoking cigarettes forever   the condition of the blessed had first made him think of becoming a saint   it was a condition based on poverty a rich poverty that impoverished his expectations   like the happy poverty of a man mowing his lawn or polishing his car   just you and the turtle wax the car beginning to gleam in the sun- shine   or thinking nothing smelling cutting grass nothing becoming a feeling opening out to everything   sat down at his typewriter like a musician at his key- board thinking maternity report   thinking his feeling sitting there might best be described by the phrase quiet joy   meditating on the major contradiction develop- ing in his report supporting paternity while denying maternity   the tentative conclusions had surprised even himself and leakage to the press caused scan- dal   government report attacks motherhood ran the headlines and now he was in big trouble   how to explain he meant that mothers too should adopt paternity as a mode   it was a matter much too subtle for the mentality of the mass media   he meant since paternity was the privileged mode mothers must assume and maternalize it   he meant paternity was the path of power while maternity operated under the sidewalks   he meant maternity was coming out from under- ground maternity approaching paternity and paternity maternity   the result would be a state of sexual fusion that might save the world   or destroy it but would certainly bypass the sexual impasse or so he predict- ed   either way resolved the contradictions the peasant crazies called the parrot and the ox   Charleen was in The Smiling Lemming eating the island specialty sweet and sad shrimp   it made her feel sweet and sad because of the spices among them hash   that was why it was expensive but feeling sweet and sad was worth it   when younger she really felt she could take over the world with her tits   now she felt even if she could so what it was all levelled out   even if she took over with tits it left the problem of the parrot-ox   the big parrot-ox was if you took it over it didn't matter what then   it didn't matter whether she made love with Tony Victor Carl Drecker or

Veronica   it didn't matter whether they loved her tits
or herself what was her self   if it didn't matter something was the matter even though they were all nice
      even though she was in love with each of them when'
she made love   she was in love when making love
making love made her fall in love   after making love
she fell out of love her lovers didn't this caused problems   she thought of it as a series it was the series that
was serious   they got stuck in repetition she'd say no I
did it with you already   or to another you can be next
confusing people and getting her into trouble   so she
tended to accumulate lovers and when she accumulated
enough she left town   she was getting close to where
she would have to leave this town unless   unless she
met someone into a similar series and got locked into a
combination   it never happened but she was optimistic it made her feel sweet and sad   sweet and sad
was beyond good and bad it bypassed the impasse the
parrot-ox   when she had finished her sweet and sad
shrimp she was reeling with feeling   it made her feel
good because that was really the best side of herself
      she wasn't bad at thinking but her gift to people was
feeling she concluded   when Veronica arrived Charleen said some people are great thinkers others are great
feelers   she told Veronica it was a category of genius
left out by the culture   she said something should be
done for the unsung feelers making people feel happy   or unhappy said Veronica Veronica was having her
own problems about just getting along   Charleen was
right she wished she had what she had temperament soul
big feelings   Veronica was very tired of big ideas ideas
were cheap the bigger the cheaper   Drecker and Carl
and Victor were full of big ideas new ones every day   big
ideas didn't help you get along they had nothing to do with
it   they made it harder you also had to get along with
the big ideas   Tony at least had no big ideas just little
ones that helped getting along   little ideas about what

to do next and how to do it that helped   she was tired
of her relation with Drecker anyway the jokes were
running out   the trouble with Tony was that he had
little ideas but also little feelings   little ideas plus little
feelings wasn't such a good combination because it got boring   Charleen had very little ideas plus very big feelings which could be a disaster   Bennett had very big
ideas and no feelings which was for Veronica even
worse   though it had its virtues here on the island
where the ideology pushed feeling   there were little
red signs hung in all the official offices that said feel
     nobody needed to tell Veronica to feel in official
offices she always felt hate   it was that tone of bureau-
cratic complacency and paternal condescension that
drove her mad   she already had a father she didn't
need others especially not government appointed
surrogates
          the whole state surrogate system sucked or
in the tongue of the peasant crazies philophallocracy fathers
fools these peasant crazies weren't so crazy thought Veronica anybody who could buy the ideology of the state surrogate system had to be stupid even though she had to admit
that the vast majority did even though it was clearly a way of
fostering a childish dependency in the population though
it was true that large segments of the population were in
fact dependent in that they had no resources it was also
true they were kept that way by the very same paternalistic
power structure the state surrogate system was designed
to support though it was not simply a question of paternal
as opposed to maternal as Carl seemed to think nor was
the resolution sororal or fraternal because the island
power structure which was nothing more than a minor
local branch of vast international financial intelligence
superpowers as Victor said could as easily take on a
maternal as a paternal form or a fraternal or sororal one or
could suddenly turn rosicrucian for that matter or vege-
tarian or buddhist or scientologist depending on current

fads which it was quick to co-opt and encourage there was nothing local superpowers liked better than riding the crest of a fad that diverted attention from itself and besides it was fun and against this what Veronica's chest filled with rage as she thought of all the tiny isolated impoverished impotent dummies including herself pissing their lives away like Tony on pointless dumb jobs or caught in the state surrogate system and what did they have as Drecker would say they had nothing against this what Veronica asked Charleen as they walked from The Smiling Lemming across Ferrell Anderson Place down Lavaggetto to The Same Thing on Wyatt where Veronica had to go enjoy herself Charleen felt differently about things she was going to be very rich when enough members of her family died off as her favorite lovers were given to understand it was the ace in her hole a consciousness of her power and of power in general and there were some things about power that Veronica didn't understand though she didn't say this to Veronica she knew that power was seedy and that super-power was superseedy and that absolute power was absolutely seedy and that seedy power ran things abso-lutely and if it didn't some other seedy power would run things absolutely and it might be seedier or even if less seedy it would still be seedy it was only a question of degrees of seediness though she had to admit of course that things could get very seedy like that fellow Hitler but she also knew that on a personal level you either had power or you didn't have power and that while power could only hollow you out only personal power could fill you up and that was why you could meet up with ragged impoverished peasant crazies who were absolutely filled with power and that was why she believed in astrology and magic and that was why she noticed with fascination the bumper stickers appearing lately around town that said hump a peasant crazy printed up no doubt by the peasant crazies who you had to admit weren't so crazy because she believed especially in the magic of sex and that was why she had been engaged so long in the pursuit of the perfect orgasm and was into techniques and even applied for a grant one time from the state surrogate system for a sex survey she was pursuing anyway grant or no grant but she was getting scared because the closer she got to perfect orgasm the more it seemed there was nothing there but an empty hole the nameless abyss she was afraid of slipping through forever she was beginning to think she had made a mistake that the perfect orgasm doesn't exist and that it takes place in a hole and that a hole is something that isn't there but is defined by what's around it so that either she was going to be constantly disappointed because there's nothing there there's only what gets you there and she should have applied for a grant to study not what it is because it isn't but what gets you there but gets you where if it isn't there or if she got there she would cease to exist because it didn't and that was why she was getting confused because if that was all there was and it wasn't there then where was it or for that matter what was it or maybe it was true as Carl liked to say that we are all figures on the ground of nothing and if so maybe it was time for a grant to look into nothing but how did you look into nothing and at times like this she really missed her children and her family and her friends and all the ties she had to cut to come here to find what she didn't have and couldn't do without but it was too late too late too late because she needed it whatever it was though she didn't say any of this to Veronica it's a matter of who controls the language said Victor in The Same Thing they were sitting at a table in front of the big plate glass window where the passersby could see Veronica enjoying herself what do you mean controlling the language Veronica laughed gaily I mean those who control the state control the language therefore the first thing to do is decontrol the language said Victor you decontrol the language by breaking the language code when you break the language code you get a new language like the tongue of the peasant crazies which they simply

call tongue in tongue for example you say break the
language code by saying loosen your tongue but loosen
your tongue also means do you want to make love
depending on the context so someone with a loose tongue
is either someone who likes to make love or someone who
has broken the language code or both Carl and Charleen
both had loose tongues that was one of the few things that
still held them together after making love they had their
friendliest and most gratifying moments they had just
made love they had just made love and were lying in one
another's arms thinking their own thoughts and feeling
peaceful and happy after a while Carl said how would you
prefer to die driving off a curve on the coast hiway listening
to really good rock she said without hesitation how would
you making love he said why can't we always be this happy
he said because it's hard to always keep your mind on
dying there are too many other problems she said if you
could keep your mind on dying maybe there wouldn't be
he said maybe not but the trouble with keeping your mind
on dying is it makes you unhappy she said there are a lot of
problems he said speaking of problems the big news was
that all their parents were planning to visit the island they
had formed a group called mom and pop or mop for short
and they were coming to the island to mop up they were
expected to pop up to mop up any day now and despite
perfunctory grumbling and the fact that it made many of
them like Charleen sick to their stomachs they were really
at heart looking forward to the visit because there were in
fact many problems for mom and pop to mop up meanwhile over in The Tartine in Camilli Lane Tony was having a
beer with Drecker Drecker knew Tony was screwing
Veronica but Tony didn't know whether Drecker knew so
Tony was being cagey so he said slowly almost like a
Chinese person so what do you think he took a slow
careful sip of his beer about what asked Drecker I don't
know about anything said Tony everybody's tired of sex
said Drecker I have it on authority there's going to be a

large asexual vote in the election oh yeah who they going to vote for asked Tony they're not going to vote for anybody they're going to abstain those who want to abstain are going to be the largest emerging unit which in a context of accelerated shatter should be substantially influential you sound like the news on TV said Tony how about playing some handball said Drecker nah I fell unlucky today I don't do anything anymore when I feel unlucky then how do you change your luck asked Drecker I wait it out said Tony I take off work and sit home with the racing sheets I bet on the horses and I buy lottery tickets when I start winning I know my luck's changing that's all when I'm feeling out of it I like to talk about things don't you think that's important asked Drecker I guess so said Tony although he didn't I like to explain things said Drecker it's like locating yourself on a map if you can't locate yourself on the map you don't know where you are if you don't know where you are you don't know where you're going or even whether you're going explaining things is like a map a kind of word map it's word radar you have to keep scanning keep talking keep explaining keep talking said Drecker what said Tony The Tartine was getting louder it was getting hard to hear keep talking said Drecker if you stop talking you're in trouble The Tartine seemed to be getting louder and louder an ocean of language was washing at his ear Hotel California was playing on the jukebox the clack of plates the click of cubes the roar of motorcycles in Camilli Lane keep talking said Drecker what said Tony Carl was getting tired of it life on the island sex exile and the thin pathos of nostalgia more and more he went down alone to The Reiser found himself at dusk staring across the pale gray wash of ocean to the horizon still slightly pastel from the sunset listening to the yap of gulls and the bellowing sea lions thinking about the failure of the last revolution after the last war the way that fraternal enthusiasm had turned into petty bourgeois nastiness of shopkeepers and the sudden appearance of large numbers of heavily armed paramilitary police at irrational intervals for no apparent reasons checking papers and making people take off their shoes the rumors about torture in the jails reports of bodies floating down the river the curious incuriosity of the students about the events of that epic month that almost brought down the republic who knows whether for better or for worse the stale directionless tone of the official culture relieved only by the clowning of the peasant crazies he was beginning to think that Victor was right for once that it was better to speak in tongue than acquiesce in what the liberal press called the responsible magnificence of contemporary culture for the thirsty millions with its concrete centers for the unexceptionable and innovation for the people he felt the need for a ridiculous saintliness with repulsive aspects to trigger a scandalous amalgam in face of the new conditions an incomprehensible baptism of lunatic poets provoking a metaphysical adolescence of abstention and fire though he was well aware there were worse things than quiet boredom and he hoped along with the others that mom and pop would put a stop to the egregious display of blockbusters afflicting the populace meanwhile he focussed attention on the increasing fre-quency of wet dog attacks although it was true you could no longer be sure whether a wet dog attack was a real wet dog attack or an undercover government wet dog attack designed to co-opt real wet dog attacks Charleen told Carl she was leaving she told Drecker she wasn't sleeping with him anymore she told Victor she wanted a divorce she sent telegrams to her seven lovers telling them not to come to the island and now she sat on a bench in The Walker and pondered the essential aloneness of everybody during the years that had followed the revolution she had believed in the essential togetherness of everybody along with every-body else but now nobody believed in the essential togetherness of everybody but while she believed in the essential aloneness of everybody she did not like to practice it because it made her lonely not only lonely from day to day but also metaphysically lonely she hoped this was one of those problems that mom and pop would pop up to mop up another alternative would be to join up with the achronician terrorists whose high spirited comraderie came from the fact they had faith in the astrological future because a collective future foils a lonely present with the fellowship of folks on the same trip which is all right as long as you don't get there meanwhile she decided she would call everybody up and tell them she changed her mind and composed a telegram to her lovers saying simply ignore previous telegram just like she had done last week and now the great day was here they all went out to the airport to meet mop winging in from the mainland with perfunctory grumbling about the impertinent tenacity of authority figures but high hopes at heart that now things would really happen that mop would clean things up or that at least they would be able to borrow some money so there they were at the landing gate flowers in hand when the old folks trooped off confused and grouchy from the long flight and frightened by the sudden change from their familiar surroundings most of them seemed to be broke and the rest held on to their money so tightly for fear of being cheated you actually had to pull it out of their hands to pay the porters and the taxis and after a while one gave up and paid oneself many of them didn't seem quite aware of where they were and one or two didn't even recognize their children above all they didn't want to be left alone and there was an undercurrent of worry that they were all going to be herded off to an old folks home some cried on their way into the city and had to be constantly reassured they kept bickering and shouting at one another and complaining about their hearts and the time change because now they didn't know when to take their pills cupped their hands over their ears yelling what what every time you said something to them were suspicious of everything and would suddenly clutch their nearest neighbor in one case the taxi driver with outbursts like no need to worry thank god now we're in good hands and indeed the children felt their obligations and did as well as they could by mom and pop feeding them and taking them for walks and putting them to bed but a mood of disappointment not to say utter depression prevailed it was certainly a case for the facilities of the state surrogate system whatever you might think of it Victor was in a pugnacious frenzy the first time he'd been in a pugnacious frenzy for a long time from arguing with his father about California Carl tried to talk to him about the 1939 Detroit Tigers but he himself could hear the mooing starting in his head Charleen was foraging in the ragged peripheries she knew the tongue saying loose tongues unleash forces but she wasn't sure she wanted to unleash them forces from the other side of the wind that bring as much ruin as rain as the peasant crazies put it forces that were invisible and insane forces that were by definition unmeasurable but which perhaps had their own measure that was the saving possibility but whether she wanted it or not she could feel that a shift was coming she could see in Carl's eyes that the bright colors were gathering in his head there was something like a change in air pressure and she knew that the weather was accumulating over the mountain in great swirls that the dikes of dichotomy were trickling tiny rivers of sand which all the bricks and balls of the financial intelligence superpowers could not shore up as the achronicians moved on the international yesno system in a battle neither could win that loose tongues would uncode the vatic structures of desire exposing the orgasm behind the orgasm and releasing seething fructive centers that would burn through the complacency of innuendo astonish the heavy stasis of lassitude and pass on in hissing diminuendos transcending disgust and exposing the nameless abyss in their wake she felt like a child the brown snout of death getting closer the death chant of the peasant crazies descending from the ancient lament of the meso-potamian hippopotamus cults intervening terminology of streets running with piss at night jukebox playing Hotel California undercover government wet dog attacks the police the smashed glass street screams running footsteps the languid switchblades the hopeless the slow grief of failure the everybody seemed to be feeling worse thought Drecker everybody except the bums outside his apartment in Casey Street they seemed to feel the same crawling out of their holes each morning looking sick and glazed staggering to the grocery for the first bottle gathering in jabbering groups pissing against walls at noon slobbering drunk in the afternoon sun panhandling and pugnacious in the mild evenings singing and dribbling snot through the night crawling back to the hole at dawn drooling vomit and head full of annihilation it was a routine repulsive and the same every day but worth thinking about a way of life something none of the exiles had managed to develop even with the help of extensive computerized time and motion studies of the kind commissioned by the local university to research the growing immigrant problem in which Victor had been a subject and on which Bennett had worked though while it was true the bums seemed to be feeling the same it was also no doubt true they were getting worse and at intervals one or another of them would simply disappear never to be seen again where was the very fat man with the red scabby face who liked to sing his terrible aria I am sick I am feeling very sick to the terraces of the cafes which responded with derisive applause and small coins or the tall thin man with the red beard and the broom talking to himself and forever uselessly sweeping the street so if the bums were feeling the same but getting worse maybe his friends were feeling worse but getting better it was worth thinking about also worth thinking about was the virtues of feeling worse as part of the larger dynamic of getting better since the worse you felt the harder you tried either that or gave up completely but in that case it could be looked at as a process of selection for the benefit of the species to the delight of the neodarwinians or even if this whole business was nonsense as was likely and there was no virtue at all in feeling worse it was worth thinking about the virtues of feeling different at least how boring it would be always to feel the same even feeling better implies feeling worse he thought about his sailboat and wondered about wind conditions all winds were swell except no winds when the wind stops you're in trouble you have to work up your own wind an interior wind what he liked to call a headwind to start things going again because if anything goes every-thing goes they were going out on the boat today he turned to Veronica sleeping in his bed and shook her shoulder let's go everything is he said Tony was real tired of fucking other people's women he figured the other people were getting tired of it too even the women were getting tired of it it was unlucky maybe he would hold out for a woman of his own who he would have to worry about other people fucking Veronica decided she agreed with Carl you had to do what was right and good only what was it Victor took Charleen down to the beach he knew Charleen was upset he was upset himself the night was warm and the moon was out they stood on the sand at the tide line and listened to the hush hush of the surf together they were all disturbed by the failure of the mop mission Carl himself was shook up when his father didn't recog-nize him it deeply disturbed his sense of the achronistic binary doubling flow of things as it had for Charleen when her father tried to bounce her on his knee again as he had done till she was seventeen and sprained his hip Charleen falling on the floor such disruptions destroy one's sense of continuity of proper descent flow without pattern is discouraging the tailwind of time needs the headwind of mind Carl was beginning to think like a peasant crazy starting to talk to his friends in twisted tongue spent most of his time alone walking the streets of Oldtown was living celibate with Charleen had stopped smoking and drinking and become unpredictable and grouchy yet his friends had begun to seek him out for advice advice he invariably refused to give saying talk does not solve problems it makes wishes wishes that sometimes come true sometimes when you don't want them to instead of giving advice he would get his friends to look into a mirror and make a wish they always came away feeling better Carl would have them look into a mirror because he said reflection is the basic human characteristic even though it gives you double trouble Carl had taken to sitting for hours in Furillo Gardens on a bench taking in its full sweep of close mowed green lawn the stands overlooking the playing field and the fine formal flower plantation different every season with in the background the well labelled botanical display of native bushes and trees with a gravel path straight as a rifle shot through the axis of the ensemble crossed by another at right angles exactly in the center where little boys sailed toy sailboats in the basin of Rickey Fountain and the orderly harmony of the whole conception its beautiful artifice in his mind made manifest many marvelous meditations on measure as a mirror managing doubling for those who found doubling troubling he had a theory that anything could be used to measure anything else as long as one thing was a conception and the other something to be conceived the mirror effect of one thing on the other making something of a nothing that would otherwise have slid by into the oblivion of the unconceived not that this nonsense made sense of anything just that the notation of its happening made him happier a sensation highly welcome in a set of synapses stretched thin to snapping and so he strolled about Oldtown heavily involved in notation of its nonsense making use of many measures according to his theory for example a mackerel to measure a monastery a labyrinth to measure an ant a feather to measure a feeling a baseball team to measure a city these are just a few illustrations the important thing being the meaning of the measure to begin with not what it is but that it is and worrying such trivia as the fact that sexual fusion results in binary fission wondering if that wasn't the parrot-ox where it all began mulling a new Eden myth god having a schizophrenic breakdown when creation moves from the pure potential of maybe to the empirical demystifications of a yesno system let there be light good night the devil's work was alienation and identity crisis polarity brings clarity not parity Charleen was meditating every morning and also every evening sometimes also in the afternoon today she got right up out of her trance looked Carl in the eye and said and now it's time to go home Carl had a certain mountain in his mind a very high mountain topped by a jagged blade of sheer rock edged with a frill of thick ice in his mind he went up that mountain made it to the top in his mind he skidded perilously on that jagged frill of ice sheer nothingness on either side of him as he walked down Boulevard Lavaggetto in the lunch crowd racing for standup shrimp salad sandwiches and crab louis so there would be time for a quick beer or a crap back up on the seventeenth floor before sitting down at the desk and the dossiers and the telephone oh lord looking in the shop windows for possible anniversary presents and already worried about forgetting mother's day as usual hoping for a swim in the lagoon this afternoon grabbing an afternoon tabloid to read over coffee the headline of which says mao mao becomes meow meow turning into The Walker wondering now he had nothing to say why everyone was coming to ask him what it was and what a relief it was finally to have nothing in his head except a kind of inflow that got caught up for a while in an interesting eddy temporary however complicated then released in an exhaust of words one way or another not unlike the exhaust stream of a jet plane twisted by random winds into illegible scribbles in the sky meanwhile Tony on the assembly line was trying to keep his mind on the production schedule while it kept trying to come back to the way Charleen's pussy felt last night like a lost dog trying to find its way home and Drecker drilling into a tooth suddenly started feeling sorry for the frowzy house-wife with her swollen jaw who had just walked into the waiting room wondering what kind of life she must have constantly harrassed by her two brats to the point where she couldn't even have a toothache without bringing them along and Veronica in The Same Thing wondering how long it would be before she could take a break stop enjoying herself and be morose for fifteen minutes and Victor was worrying about Charleen and what was going on in the still black pool of her consciousness and wondering whether she knew and Charleen was thinking about Victor's relation with Bennett whether it made him happy poor Victor and Veronica was feeling sorry for Carl because he seemed so isolated and lonely even though he said he liked it that way which maybe was true though she couldn't understand why if so and Drecker was feeling sorry for everybody convinced that nobody would ever get anything straightened out and Tony was feeling sorry for himself because he had to spend the rest of the day on the dumb assembly line thinking what a way to spend your life and thinking more and more that his death would have no meaning and Carl was walking across Ferrell Anderson Place hoping for the best he was beginning to get the hang of the native dialect finally he went into The Smiling Lemming and put his elbow on the bar gimme a serious he said to the bartender the bartender grunted drew a large beer and put it down in front of Carl so what about dese guys said Carl the bartender gave him a hard look wha da game he said yeah da game said Carl a lump a shid said the bartender you tink so said Carl kemmon whadda you tawkin dese schmucks said the bartender you seen whaddey dun lasnight inna second whaddafuck you tawkin about said the bartender he was going red in the face whaddja lose money said Carl money said the bartender yafuckinass I drop ten said the bartender an widdis joik taday dey oughta sendim back ta Detrert om tellinya said the bartender a man in tweeds and waxed moustache came up to the bar ah I beg your pardon he said is your name Carl no said Carl all the same I'd like to put something to you if you don't mind to what question is man the answer he asked that's the riddle of the shrinks said Carl he spit on the floor and walked out by jove I'd give one hundred bricks for that chap's insight said the man in tweeds the new conditions were not jumping to any conclusions out on Ferrell Anderson Place as Carl picked his way through the crowd Boulevard Lavaggetto was full of loose ends and The Campanella was ringing he stopped to watch a pick-up basketball game in Robinson Square Park then cut across Amoros Avenue to Edwards Alley when he thought he saw the agent following him so drifted down Head to Zimmer and lost himself in the labyrinth of streets in Oldtown now so familiar to him left on Drysdale Mews right on Duroucher Row left on Barney Walk through Hodges Court in and out of Gilliam Impasse around Craig Crescent to Labine Lane and out through Hoak Terrace and Snider Drive knowing that sooner or later he would end up in the kiosk in Reese Park or more likely on The Reiser watching the ships go out with the tide and thinking it was time to go and then reminding himself as he had to every time that he was already going had always been going that there was never any question of staying however much that might have seemed to be the case the sunlight winking on the wavelets but as usual in the afternoon the clouds gathering over Mt. Medwick and

at a certain hour he would drift over toward The Tartine in
Camilli Lane and then he might remember that he had
promised to visit Veronica enjoying herself in The Same
Thing on Wyatt and on the way he would maybe notice the
turn of the century style of the buildings around Stanky
and Cox so interesting under their ugly black coating of
soot or wander into an old print shop on Hermanski
Square hoping to add to his collection of antique orange
wrappings or he might meet Victor on The Walker and sit
with him on a bench feeding the local population of the
island's peculiar breed of black long eared squirrels of
which Victor was so fond while the day petered peacefully
out in the gray afternoon drizzle smudging the outlines of
the ancient city as he went walking off down The Walker
noting moisture beading on black umbrellas the overhead
fillagree of trees starting to leaf the muffled roar of distant
motors the hiss of a bicycle the click of a boot the sway of a
haunch the rose of a cheek the clunk of a car door closing a
pigeon flopping gracelessly by the sculpted hairdo of a
demoiselle the texture of a pastry tart in a store window the
feel of a city street in the rain and all the other cheap thrills
of the afternoon but wishing they hadn't demolished the
old public toilets because he had to piss a fact more
fundamental than a fund of ephemeral epiphanies but
reflecting that all things come to an end at the same time
recognizing there was no point imposing a sense of
tragedy on old public toilets and that things didn't have
beginnings and endings in that sense they just start and
then they stop

FICTION COLLECTIVE
Books in Print: